PER-BAST

A TALE OF CATS IN ANCIENT EGYPT

Lara-Dawn Stiegler

Per-Bast: A Tale of Cats in Ancient Egypt

Copyright © 2014 Lara-Dawn Stiegler

www.laradawn.com

http://www.perbast.com

Published by
Published by Kielo Publishing, Vancouver

ISBN 978-0-9781793-1-1

Printed and bound in the United States of America

Second Edition

To Mom,
Who always encouraged me to follow my dreams
and trust my heart.

* Special thanks to Rebecca Sanders, Eb Mills, and
Katie Ellison for all of your help and support in
preparing this manuscript.

Contents

Author's Notes

AN ELEGANT STATUE of a seated cat sits in a museum and commands the attention of visitors. Around her neck rests an amulet of a winged scarab holding up the rising sun. The story behind that statue has faded from living memory; the sculptor's hand is now but mere bone; his tools are prized artefacts; and the cat, from which that statue was inspired, long ago transversed the paths of the ancient Egyptian underworld.

This is the tale that breathes to life that age-old sculpture. The story takes place during the thirty-first year of the reign of Ramses III, during a period known as the New Kingdom—Egypt's second Golden Age. Whereas the feline characters are of course fictional, most of the humans mentioned existed in antiquity: Ramses III, his Vizier Ta, and Tiye, a wife of the pharaoh.

The myths and scrolls mentioned are historical and serve as the framework for this story—except for the feline lineages and their histories, which are all invented. While I have striven for historical accuracy, I have also framed this story from the point of view of the ancient Egyptians, who believed that magic and deities played a personal role in their everyday lives.

In the ancient Egyptian language, the word per simply meant "house" as in "city," as cities were constructed around temples, which were considered the houses of gods. For this story, I've broadened this word's meaning to also signify "house" as in a lineage. Such as with the feline lineage of "Per-Mafdet", it would literally mean "house of Mafdet."

CHAPTER 1

Upon the Wings of Horus

*The past has been rolled into a scroll I shall
not see again.*

~BOOK OF THE DEAD

THE SUN SET the air on fire.

Incense permeated a dry midday wind. The land lay voiceless as death until the first cries of mourners pierced the silence. A sarcophagus passed into sight, gilded in gold and resting upon a funeral barge pulled across the land by a pair of brown oxen.

A bald man in a white robe escorted the procession. The skin of a leopard hung over his back. His hands gripped a silver ankh—the symbol of everlasting life. This newly-appointed high priest walked on, solemnly leading his predecessor's mummified body towards its house of eternity.

Behind the funeral barge trailed the mourners: women who wailed above the prayers and chants uttered by the priests. They tore at their hair, shed tears of sorrow, and threw ash upon their bodies. Servants followed closely behind. They carried a chest upon which sat a statue of the jackal god Anubis, guardian of the dead and their tombs. Rays of sunlight pounded the statue's sleek ebony and gold casing. Within the chest were personal items of the deceased and canopic jars containing his preserved internal organs; all were meant to last forever.

Upon a rooftop sat a cat. From her vantage point she watched the funeral. Her pupils had reduced to slits to keep out the harsh glare of the sun. Like the surface of the Nile, her green eyes glistened. A powerful river of memories flowed through her mind and touched her heart. She could see the high priest Akhotep as he was in life, the temple he had served in, and the cats with whom he had shared his life.

Her memory rested upon the image of a cat named Sahu, whose fur held a sheen of tarnished silver. The words *I promise I will always be there for you* echoed in her mind. Swiftly she shut out her affections and focused instead on the funeral procession. The sarcophagi of mummified cats came into sight. Neferure turned sharply away, bitterly wondering if the promise of 'being there' included resting in a dark tomb far beneath the earth.

Onwards strode the procession, toward the Nile where the priests, the mourners and the servants would all board boats and make their way towards the West Bank of Thebes. There the sun would set, behind the tombs of the dead. Akhotep's spirit had already been taken upon the wings of the god Horus and judged before Osiris in the realm of Amenti, the land of the dead. His heart had been placed on the scales in the hall of Two-Truths and by the power of

Anubis weighed against a single feather. The same had been done with the hearts of the cats to be buried with him.

Neferure knew tales of the lands through which the departed passed on their quest for eternal life. The afterworld was filled with peril and hardship before one reached peace within the reed fields of Aaru. Sahu had always been a survivor, but would he pass the tests of the gods? Would the scales tip to his demise? His fate was a secret that dreams would not tell.

She reached for his presence, always just beyond her grasp. It never left but was never seen, as though lying in a tomb of buried hopes. She could have passed through all the gates of Thebes and none would have led to where she needed to go. It was as though she were living in two worlds. Dying where there was no death, living where there was no life.

She had paced the ruins of Akhotep's house after the fire, not knowing what she searched for. An explanation, perhaps. Why had the gods torn Sahu away so suddenly, so unjustly? Among the cold ashes she had found no answers. The shadow of Sahu's pain and fear as he burned alive or suffocated in smoke had caused her to shudder.

A noise below refocused her attention.

Neferure looked down, swivelling her ears, surprised to see the pharaoh and his guards. Ramesses III stood still and silent, intensely watching the funeral procession. A striped nemes cloth draped over his head, gathered at the back and ran down behind his ears. It made his face a mirror image of the gold cast cobra rearing upon his brow. An intricate usekh collar, with its many rows of coloured and golden beads, rested upon his broad shoulders. His muscles, forged through years of war, stood strong despite years of extravagance. His face was lined by the cares of a kingdom to rule.

A man unknown to Neferure approached the pharaoh. His pleated white linen garb and finery suggested he held high social standing. The captain of the guard blocked his way until the pharaoh waved the stranger through.

The stranger stopped and bowed before Ramesses. 'My king, may life, health, and strength be given unto you.'

Ramesses bade the man to rise. Concern etched into the pharaoh's strong features. 'What is it that brings you from so far, Qetu?'

Qetu rose. 'I know you have always respected my decisions as the vizier of Lower Egypt; thus you must also understand my method of reasoning. I would not have come in person had I not felt it necessary. Words take too long to travel up and down the Nile.'

Neferure, with her keen feline eyes, watched the frown upon Ramesses' face deepen. 'Does this deal with the problem you wrote of earlier?'

'Yes.' Qetu met Ramesses' hard gaze. 'It is spreading.'

'Could it be a plague of the goddess Sekhmet? Have we angered the great lioness goddess, the eye of Ra?'

'Quite possibly. This plague is linked to the spread of vermin. If it follows the same pattern here as in the delta, then we will see the cats affected first. It won't take long to pass to the people.'

Neferure perked her ears and drew her head forward. Her muscles tensed at the thought of disease spreading among her kind. She wished she could question the vizier further, yet few could converse with animals. Being a representative on earth of the gods, the pharaoh could do this, but Neferure doubted this was so about the vizier.

'Very well,' Ramesses replied. 'Increase the offerings and hymns at all of Sekhmet's temples.'

'I have already done so.'

Ramesses looked away and towards the horizon. For a while he was silent, as if waiting for an answer to come from the mouth of Amun-Ra himself. 'This problem will not be so easily solved. Such a poor time it is for these evils. I have repelled all foreign invaders, but funds are low and the crops are failing. Many of the tomb builders of the West Bank have gone on strike, and those who deliver their rations are not doing so as promised. Qetu, the gods surely are angry at us. We must find out why. Perhaps I am to blame, for I may have sought too hard to be more than Ramesses the Great. The gods may have judged me as overreaching.'

'I assure you, my king, that you are loved and respected among those in Egypt and in Amenti. This plague is surely not of your doing.'

'Very well. Return to your proper place and oversee further offerings to Sekhmet. I will speak to the gods, and when I find an answer you will hear of it.'

Qetu paused for a moment before replying. To Neferure's eyes he seemed irked. 'I shall depart in a few days, when the boats are ready.' He paused again. 'If I may ask, why did you not lead the funeral yourself?'

'I decided to give that chance to Khesef-hra.'

'Does he not make a fine high priest?'

'Yes,' Ramesses said, 'so far he has done admirably.'

Silence again.

Qetu broke it. 'My lord, I will help make Egypt healthier and more prosperous than ever before. You may put your full faith in that.'

Ramesses looked at him and gave a slight smile. He then dismissed the vizier. Qetu bowed and nodded his head, then headed towards the river.

By the time Neferure returned to her home, the pale glow of twilight had enveloped the land. She wondered when the plague would strike in Thebes and how it would affect the lives of cats. Surely it would hit the strays before the house-cats. They were always first affected by any disease or hardship. The high priest Akhotep, who was meant to cleanse the land, had died just prior to the plague. Coincidence, or something more sinister? An ominous feeling haunted her, telling of a deeper evil lying beneath the surface of recent events. Her mind raced searching for answers, desperate for a morsel of reason for the high priest's death—and Sahu's. All she found were doubts and a world that had moved on while she was left behind, wandering between the lands of the living and the dead.

She sat in her garden, on the edge of a grand rectangular pool. Lotuses rested upon the still waters, their blue and white flowers submerged for the night. Ornamental fish swam beneath the surface, amongst the lotus roots, taunting her to catch them.

An evening breeze wafted through the garden, laced with the scent of the many jasmine flowers bordering the pool. Sycamore and pomegranate trees were planted in rows, their shade greatly revered during the heat of the day. Two willow trees stood before the pool; their many thin branches hung like a living curtain over the water and earth. The soil here was rich with memories of Neferure's youth.

The next morning she would visit Heqaib. He would surely have something to say about the plague. More importantly, she wanted to know what he thought would happen to Sahu's spirit. Heqaib had known Sahu even before she had. It was he who had come to her, some forty days ago, and told her what she never wanted to hear. Neferure wanted to visit Heqaib that very night, but he was getting on in years, and he was odd in that he preferred sunlight over moonlight. He was an unusual cat in many ways.

Neferure passed through the garden, her paws deftly trotting over grass and dirt, until she came to the entrance hall of her home. It was the estate wherein lived Ta, the vizier of Upper Egypt.

Only the palaces of the pharaoh bested the estate. As with all houses of the living, it was built of mud brick. Only the dwellings of the gods or the resting places of spirits were built of stone. The house walls were plastered white and bore colourful images of marshes with fish and lotuses, flying birds, deities, and events of day-to-day life. Wooden columns supporting the ceiling were carved at the top to resemble the lotus flower—the symbol of Upper Egypt.

Furniture was sparse and elaborate, inlaid with gold, silver and electrum, and crafted by some of the finest artisans of Egypt.

Recessed into the wall to Neferure's right was the typical household shrine. It held statues of the gods worshipped by the house's inhabitants. One of the largest statues was that of a cat. Ta's wife, Hatia, was a patron of the goddess Bast, and her strong devotion was evident in the elaborate gold statue she had commissioned.

Neferure took a long look at the seated, proud, and dignified image of the feline goddess—an image that bore such a likeness to herself. Hatia often spoke of seeing the essence of Bast shine through all cats and how some carried themselves as though they were deities on earth.

Now Hatia was standing before her prized statue of Bast, holding a small child bundled in linen in her arms. Black kohl lined her eyes, matching the colour of the sleek hair that framed her face and fell just short of her shoulders. Her arms and neck bore gold jewellery of serpents and winged scarabs. The soft candlelight from the shrine danced upon the faces of both mother and child. Hatia was asking for protection for herself and her newborn son.

'Bast,' Hatia said in a whisper, 'great goddess of the sun, protectress of cats, of children, and of Egypt, please guard my new child as you would your own.'

After placing an amulet of a cat around the boy's neck, Hatia retreated from the entrance hall. Neferure had already asked Bast for any dream of significance to the answers she sought, so she now followed the wisps of linen trailing behind as Hatia walked. Soon they entered a stately room filled with carved columns, murals, and exquisite furniture—the grand hall of the estate.

Grooming herself upon a chair was Takhaet. She was of a fine and delicate build. Hardly ever did she choose to set foot outside. Neferure attributed this to the wind: she figured it would both ruffle Takhaet's fur and pick her up off her feet. Takhaet's markings looked as though they had been washed away by the annual flood, giving her a muted, yet elegant, pastel appearance. Contrasted against Neferure's bold markings set upon fur coloured like aged gold, one would never guess they were sisters. When Takhaet finished grooming her left shoulder, at last seeming satisfied with her appearance, she looked over at Neferure as if knowing what was on her sister's mind.

'He was born a stray,' Takhaet said, referring to Sahu. 'Just be thankful he didn't die as one. I hear a cat of Per-Maahes will be arriving here in Thebes tomorrow, by boat. That lineage is supposed to be—'

Neferure narrowed her eyes. 'Don't you realize there's something wrong with all of this?'

'Yes, strays, even former ones, should not have proper burials.' Takhaet looked at her paw, scrutinizing its appearance. 'Strays are strays because they must have angered the gods. The gods can see what is in their souls. If they were ousted by the gods then surely they should be ousted by us as well.'

'I speak of the human they're burying. When I last saw Akhotep he seemed oddly worried. Both Sahu and I noticed it. Sahu said he would follow Akhotep around the temple to see if he could find the source of his unease. Now, both are...'

'Dead?'

'Yes.' Neferure looked down.

'Then you're connecting these two events?' Takhaet asked, in a tone suggesting she didn't care to hear the answer.

'I am.'

Takhaet straightened out a single hair on her paw. 'You don't think you're simply trying to give Sahu's end a just cause? I find Akhotep's death quite plausible. Simply, he died because it was his time to die. Being old, and likely forgetful, he left a lantern burning as he fell asleep, and one of the cats, maybe even Sahu, knocked it over while chasing a moth. A fire started, and Akhotep died of smoke inhalation while trying to escape. End of story.'

Exasperated by her sister's incessant careless attitude towards the suffering of others, Neferure repressed the budding reprimand she knew would fail to change Takhaet's ways. 'I don't believe it was that simple. When I went to investigate, I did see a lantern, but I did not see any remains of a scroll, nor could I smell any burned papyrus. I doubt Akhotep would have left the lantern lit if he hadn't been reading. The doorway was scorched the most, as if the fire started there. And why was Akhotep rushed to be mummified in only forty days when he could have afforded the full seventy-day procedure? Now I hear talk of a coming plague. The vizier of Lower Egypt himself came to deliver the news. He said the plague will hit us first and then the humans. Doesn't it seem odd that all these events are coinciding? There is some deeper evil behind it. I know there is.'

Takhaet swished her tail in annoyance. 'As usual I don't agree with you. Although I will accept your opinion as your own, I ask you to promise me one thing: to not waste your time trying to solve mysteries that aren't there.'

'I can't make that promise. I would be betraying Sahu's memory if I didn't find out what he died for.' Neferure stood proud and narrowed her eyes. 'Unlike you, I couldn't live with that.'

'Suit yourself. You always have.' Takhaet straightened her posture, jumped off the chair and daintily walked away with her head and tail held high in the air. A few paces from the doorway she looked back. 'You know, curiosity will be the death of you.'

CHAPTER 2

Heqaib

BLOSSOMS OF ORANGE light floated upon the Nile as the brightness of Amun-Ra ascended from beyond the hills in the east. Upon his solar barque he sailed through the clouds with his crew of gods and goddesses, those who helped him defeat the terrible serpent Apep every night. Victorious again over his greatest enemy, Amun-Ra could bring light and order to the lands for another day.

A sacred ibis skimmed the river's surface and landed smoothly upon the marsh. He blended in among the congregation of his kind. All had white bodies and wing feathers tipped with the same intense black that coloured their long legs, necks and beaks. They were ever alert, gazing intently at all of life. The air was buzzing with their dialogue, theories about the universe, the latest news from the Delta, and the unravelling of ancient mysteries. It was no wonder Thoth, the god of wisdom, writing, and science, frequently appeared as an ibis.

Neferure turned away from that sight, squeezed under several low growing shrubs, and entered Heqaib's home.

Heat and light diminished as she passed through the

13

doorway. Neferure's acute eyes adjusted easily to the dimness. Rough reed mats lined the floor, keeping dust from rising. The whole dwelling was much smaller than any one room in her own house. A single window, placed high up in the wall and facing the north, allowed for some light and gave the place a subdued atmosphere. She looked up at the household shrine set into the wall. There stood intricately carved statues of Amun-Ra, his wife, Mut, and their child Khonsu, the gods honoured at Thebes. Also present was a statue of Thoth, appearing as a man with the head of an ibis, for she was inside the house of a scribe.

The area behind Thoth's statue held more than just shadows. Neferure looked closer and noticed a ball of fur hunched over and motionless. Heqaib had squeezed into a crevice, trying to hide himself. Neferure was not so easily fooled, but neither did Heqaib wish her to be. He only meant to avoid the scribe who lived in his house.

'I see you've managed to steal another text,' she said.

Startled, Heqaib turned and bumped into the statue of Amun-Ra. The statue teetered uneasily back and forth. Immediately he sat still and groomed his paw, acting as if nothing happened.

Neferure desperately tried not to show any sign of amusement, knowing Heqaib always wished to hold himself with a quiet dignity. Grace was something he wasn't built for, and that was a fact best not dwelt upon. She quickly moved the conversation along.

'Please tell me you've been outside this room in the past few days.'

'The world can wait,' Heqaib replied. 'I can only hide

this document for so long before someone finds it and takes it away.' He glanced over at a scroll he'd left in the shadows. 'There are always greater depths to be uncovered and more meanings to be deciphered.' A vacant glaze came over his eyes as he drifted back into thought.

'Well, it's comforting to know some things in life remain unchanged.' Heqaib drew his ears back, annoyed to be torn from his inner world. His eyes softened soon after. 'For me, the most change happens right here in this room.'

Neferure looked up and down the plastered walls and around the scantly decorated house. She couldn't find anything that had been changed in ages.

'Just today I finished deciphering another story.' Heqaib's excitement showed as for once his monotone voice varied in pitch. 'I've gained a whole new batch of knowledge about Isis.'

'A whole tale can be stored on a single piece of papyrus?' Neferure asked.

'Yes. The hieroglyphs all tell stories. Nothing written is without meaning.'

Neferure sat down and began carefully grooming her tail. For once she wanted to know what interested Heqaib so much about the world of images and scrolls. His story might at least distract her from the burden her heart carried. She looked up. 'Tell me, what does it say?'

Heqaib's eyes widened and his ears perked forward. A long time must have passed since he'd been asked for knowledge. 'It speaks the story of how Isis learned Amun-Ra's secret name.'

'Secret name?'

'If anyone ever learned it, they could use it in any magical spell and gain power over Amun-Ra. The name was given to him upon his birth and never uttered since. No one but he knew it.'

'Until Isis.'

'Exactly.' Heqaib grabbed the papyrus paper in his mouth and placed it before him. He pressed it down with his paw and referred to it throughout the story.

Isis, Great of Magic, was the smartest and wisest of the gods. She was also clever, cunning, and eloquent of speech. She knew all there was to know—all except for Ra's secret name. Knowing as much as she did, Isis was well aware of the importance hidden within his true name. In time she set her heart upon finding it.

'She fashioned a snake, unlike any other, from the soil beneath her feet. She then placed it upon a path Ra walked daily during his earthly reign as pharaoh. Before long, Ra was bitten by the snake. He turned deathly ill. He cried out to the heavens, and all the gods came to his aid.

'Since the poison was unknown, none could help him. Ra shivered as a force more painful than fire coursed through his body. It was then that Isis came forth. With her cleverness and knowledge she convinced Ra that his true name must be uttered in her spell if it were to cure him.

'Despite his immense pain, Ra attempted to give her many of his other titles. Isis, wise as she was, knew none of them was the one she sought. She continued to persuade and Ra continued to suffer. Eventually she obtained his secret name. Ra transferred it from his own heart into

hers. True to her word, Isis used the name in her spell and rid the poison from Ra's body.'

Heqaib ended the story.

Questions spun in Neferure's mind. 'Did Isis give the name to anyone else?'

'Only her son, the falcon god Horus.'

Neferure got up and silently paced around the room. She thought of Amenti, the realm of the dead. She thought of the green fields of Aaru and the Nile eternally flowing through the heart of that land. At that very moment Sahu could be stalking birds at the edge of a marsh, waiting for the day when she would appear through the reeds, or else his soul could have been sent into darkness.

She wanted her heart put to rest. 'I came for a few reasons. First, I want to know what happened to Sahu when he died. I want to know if he passed the weighing of the heart ceremony.'

Heqaib set his eyes to the text, though they did not focus upon it. 'Not all knowledge is written on walls or on a sheet of papyrus. I can't tell you what happened to Sahu. I can only say I would rest my name on the likelihood his heart passed.'

'I don't understand why you can't find out.' Neferure stopped pacing and looked directly at Heqaib. 'If records are written about the doings of the gods then surely they're also written about the judgement of those who passed on.'

'Those records are written, but it is done by Thoth, and they are kept in the underworld, in Amenti.' Heqaib took a deep breath before continuing. 'What else was it you wanted to ask me?'

'Only what you know of the circumstances surrounding Akhotep's death. You sneak through the temple sometimes, looking for scrolls.' Heqaib glanced about nervously. 'I know you do, but I don't care. I only want to know if you noticed anything odd.'

'I wasn't looking out for anything odd,' Heqaib said. 'To be honest I'm never really observant about the world around me. When I read, everything else fades away, and when I walk I contemplate what I've recently read.'

'Don't you think Akhotep's death was rather mysterious and his burial quick?' Neferure didn't wait for Heqaib to answer. 'On the same day he was buried, the vizier from Lower Egypt came all the way here to bring news of an impending plague. He says it's moving southwards, carried by mice, and it will spread first to the cats.'

'The vizier is behind in his news. I heard yesterday from Ahmes that a plague hit the strays.'

Neferure glanced at the doorway. 'It won't take long before it starts affecting us.'

'Knowing most strays, they'll want to help it along.' Heqaib tensed. 'Oh, I'm sorry.' he quickly added. 'Pretend I didn't say that.'

'I'll pretend you only thought it. Thank you for your help.'

Neferure straightened her tail and turned to leave. She'd heard an interesting story, but that was all. Whatever Akhotep may have discovered still eluded her, and Heqaib knew nothing of what went on in Amenti. All his studies were to do with things beyond sight, yet when it came down to what really mattered, he knew nothing.

She felt angry with Sahu. If his heart did pass the weighing ceremony, why did he not come and tell her so? The voices of the dead had been known, on occasion, to speak with the living. Mortal sight could not always see beyond realms, but the heart, the seat of the soul, could know truths logic could not convey. Why did her heart tell her nothing? She had no clue to how Sahu fared in his quest for eternal life. His promise meant nothing in life or death.

'Wait!' Heqaib said. 'There is one thing, however small it may be, which might be of use to you.' Neferure spun around in her tracks. 'Akhotep had in his possession some texts he was reading intently before he died. I intended to grab them for myself, as I'd never read them. After his death I went to look for those texts, but they were gone. They may have perished with him in the fires.'

Neferure gave this some thought. 'To know you hadn't read them, you must have seen what they were about.'

'I only know because they smelled as though they hadn't been read *or needed* in a long time. Dust still lingered upon them.' Heqaib paused. 'Watch out. While looking, I was nearly attacked by a burly cat with copper-tipped fur, a stray I believe, who was lurking outside the temple.

'Mehen?'

'I don't know, but I hear rumours of his presence in the area.'

'Thank you, Heqaib. I will be watchful.' Her thoughts dwelt on one fact: all trails led to Mehen. She might need to confront him for answers despite the danger inherent in approaching such a notorious stray. With little else to say, Neferure turned and exited the house, glad to be back outdoors where the air flowed freer.

Many cats were awake and about. Some stood on their roofs, looking towards the river, while others were heading directly to the great temple of Karnak.

She sat for a time outside Heqaib's house, watching the steady stream of cats pass by. The streets in that area were smaller and the houses crammed much closer together than in her own neighbourhood. Livelier and noisier, it contrasted with the quiet and tranquil atmosphere of her home, where she often felt despondent since Sahu's death.

'Neferure!' A familiar voice broke into her thoughts. Turning around, she caught sight of Ahmes, who predictably gripped a mouse in her mouth. Around Ahmes's neck glinted an usekh collar with two rows of stone beads, one of pale-green serpentine and the other of alabaster. Each row of stones was interspersed with a row of gold beads. In the centre of her collar rested an amulet of emerald and gold, shaped as a winged serpent. She was of Per-Mafdet, a lineage of cats who served royalty as protectors from snakes, scorpions, and vermin.

'Good catch.' Neferure looked at the mouse hanging limply from Ahmes's mouth. 'Where's this one going?'

Ahmes set her mouse down. 'This one is for that pleasant man in the small house over to your left. He's the one who served me part of his dinner after I killed a snake hiding under his table, remember?'

'Yes,' Neferure recalled.

'He really enjoyed the last mouse, shouted for joy when he stepped on it. Now I'm going to leave him another.'

'Not to be rude, but aren't you supposed to be protecting the pharaoh from snakes and scorpions instead?'

'True, but I have to hone my skills somehow. Three days have passed since there's been a mouse at the palace and twelve since I've even caught the smell of a snake.' Ahmes looked down at the mouse, then towards the eastern hills. 'Got to hurry, the sun has risen. No fun if it isn't a surprise.'

Ahmes picked up her prey trotted off towards the house. Neferure sat quietly, gazing at the sun as it rose among the houses, washing away the shadows. Light glittered upon buildings, people and their golden jewellery, detailing the world before her eyes. Slowly a trance took hold. The landscape around her clouded over, and all her eyes beheld was a faint river of light flowing forwards from beneath the sun. Trapped and powerless, Neferure strained to bring the world back in focus. Panic gripped her heart and sent it racing

A deep yell pounded into the silence, echoing through Neferure's thin ears, tearing her from her trance.

Quick as a scorpion strikes, Ahmes bolted out of the house, chased by an angry man hopping on one foot and muttering to himself about foul beasts of the underworld. Tail puffed out, Ahmes hid behind Heqaib's doorway.

The man took awhile to leave. Perhaps, Neferure figured, he felt the more he shook his fist at Heqaib's doorway, the more his point would be made. People walking down the streets gave him a wide berth. A few children pointed at him, whispered to each other, and giggled. His wife came outside, and upon seeing his display she shaded her face with her hand and quickly disappeared indoors. When at last the man gave up and returned to his home, he nearly stumbled over a few cats heading towards Karnak. More muttering about his ruined day ensued as he returned to the house.

When he was a safe distance away, Ahmes cautiously returned to where Neferure was seated.

'He didn't seem so happy about that,' Neferure remarked.

Ahmes sat down. With pupils dilated round as her face, and ears flatter than a plank, she watched the man pour water over his foot. Neferure figured Ahmes was giving thought as to what she did wrong, wondering what she herself wouldn't have liked about the situation. Meanwhile, more cats were emerging from their homes and walking towards the temple. They chattered a great deal. People walking up and down the streets stopped and watched the streams of cats heading northwards.

'That's it!' Ahmes declared. 'Maybe he was mad because I didn't let him kill it himself. That must be it. I'll make it up to him next time by delivering a mouse that is still alive.'

Her memory may be as sharp as her claws, Neferure thought, *but she understands less about humans than Takhaet does about the outdoors.*

'Ahmes, I want to say something.'

'You can tell me anything.'

'First,' Neferure said, 'just know that you're not likely to believe me. I'm asking you now, as my best friend, to please hear me out and try to see my words as reason.'

With great care Neferure explained her theory that Akhotep's death and the coming plague were connected. As the words surfaced they sounded to her as though they were ridiculous; nevertheless, she finished voicing her opinion. Ahmes listened with patience, but a look of pity grew upon her face.

'Neferure.' Ahmes hesitated. 'I mean it with good intentions when I say that for once I think your sister is right. You're searching too hard for something that isn't there.'

An awkward silence hung between them. Who was there to turn to when even Ahmes wouldn't believe her? The chattering in the street died down as the last of the cats walked out of sight. A few people shrugged their shoulders before moving on.

Neferure looked towards Karnak. 'As the pharaoh's cat, it's probably your job to greet this initiate of Per-Maahes.'

Ahmes's eyes lit up and her muscles coiled, gathering power. She paused in mid leap. 'Why don't you come along? It'll provide you with some distraction.'

Hesitantly, Neferure agreed. Normally she would have been curious and looking forward to such a momentous occasion, but now all she wanted were answers to her questions.

CHAPTER 3

Per-Maahes

'I CAN SEE it! White sails on the horizon!'

The heavy silence among the cats broke. A boat approached, driven up the Nile by a large square sail capturing the northern wind. High above a hawk circled in the sky, as if guiding the boat to its destination. With everlasting patience the cats waited at the entrance to Karnak Temple, standing as still as stone sphinxes.

The golden tops of Queen Hatshepsut's red granite obelisks caught the morning light of Amun-Ra. The obelisks all shone as beacons, lighting the house of the sun god.

The boat turned leisurely into the canal. Waves washed upon the prow as it the oarsmen rowed into the quay and docked in front of the temple. An avenue flanked on both sides by ram-headed sphinxes and low growing shrubs lead from the boat to the high-walled entrance into Karnak.

People on the shore secured the boat to the dock with ropes and attached a ramp. A few priests stepped off and made their way down the avenue towards the temple, surveying the large gathering of cats.

A noblewoman of regal bearing disembarked. She

walked down the avenue with a sensual flow that transfixed her retinue of soldiers. Four handmaidens carrying
the woman's possessions trailed behind.

The noblewoman stopped, turned, and drew her thick
braided hair off of her alabaster smooth face. 'Pyhia,
Itakayt, and Seshemetka. Please take my effects back to my
chambers, and tell my son Pentawer that I have returned.
Kesi, you are to accompany me to court tonight.'

'Yes my lady,' Kesi replied.

'Court?' Neferure asked. 'Who is that woman? I know
I've seen her before.'

'Which one? The noblewoman? That is Tiye,' Ahmes
replied. 'You should visit the palace more often. She's
one of Ramesses' royal wives. She was visiting relatives in
Piramesses. Ramesses will be delighted by her return.'

As the human procession moved away from the boat,
the gathering of cats swept their gazes over the deck, looking for a sign. First there was nothing, and then there was
a glimmer of gold.

He was slighter of build than Neferure imagined someone of Per-Maahes would be and much younger than
anyone must have expected. Nevertheless, he strode off the
boat with his head and tail high in the air. Proudly he wore
his usekh collar. It consisted of two rows of beads, one of
carnelian and the other of a golden-orange topaz. Just as
with Ahmes's collar, the rows of stones were interspersed
with rows of golden beads. A striking red garnet amulet
carved as the udjat, the eye of Horus, was centred upon
his neck. He had not fully grown into his adornment, and
it looked a burden to him. Neferure supposed he would

greatly need the protection and strength the amulet offered.

A kitten bounded up to a cat sitting near Neferure and leapt on top of a ram-headed sphinx statue to find a better view. He looked at the young cat of Per-Maahes with wide eyes. 'Who's he?'

'He is of Per-Maahes.' The mother cat's eyes tracked the adolescent cat as he strode past the captivated onlookers. 'They mirror the essence of the lion-god Maahes, who helps Amun-Ra battle the serpent Apep. They are a fierce and protective lineage of cats who defend the weak and punish those who do not hold true to the essence of Ma'at—order, truth, and justice. Only the finest are chosen to uphold the lineage.'

The young kitten stared in wonder. 'He looks barely older than me.' To this his mother said nothing. 'Does Per-Bast exist?' he asked.

'No. No one has yet done anything worthy enough to found the lines of the great cat goddess. One day it may be declared.' The kitten's mother then looked towards Ahmes. 'However, there is a cat of Per-Mafdet here in Thebes. They protect the pharaoh from dangerous snakes and scorpions, and guard the temples from mice and rats.'

'What of Per-Sekhmet?' the kitten asked.

'They are lions who can invoke the deadly powers of Sekhmet. They walk with the pharaohs and destroy their enemies. The history of their lineage is so ancient it has been lost.'

'What does their usekh collar look like?'

'They wear the amulet of a rearing serpent—the uraeus, in front of the solar disc.'

Neferure turned her attention away from the kitten's history lesson. Ahmes moved to the end of the avenue, in the shadow of Karnak Temple, to greet the new arrival. Neferure's curiosity urged her to follow.

The cat of Per-Maahes wasted no time in making his way directly to Karnak. He strode down the avenue of ram-headed sphinxes. Between each statue's paws stood a figure of Ramesses the Great. The cat's self-assured gait suggested he had ambitions in life as high as the pharaoh guarding his path. The sun shone above the temple, among the many obelisks, and upon his garnet amulet.

Ahmes and Neferure stood near the temple gateway, off to the side. Behind them rose the first of many pylons. Each of the two mountainous walls gradually sloped inward at the sides. Images and hieroglyphics painted in an array of stunning colours and shades covered the whole of the pylon walls. Shadows of the billowing flags above played as waves upon the ground. Neferure drew a deep breath; the last time she sat outside the temple walls, Sahu was with her.

'Greetings,' a strong voice sounded. Neferure was surprised to see the cat of Per-Maahes standing directly in front of Ahmes. She must have drifted in thought. 'I am Khakhati, son of Djah, the daughter of Khu, descendant of Ibenre and Nakhti, founders of Per-Maahes.'

'I—'

Neferure was cut short. 'Who might you be?' Khakhati asked Ahmes.

'I'm Ahmes—'

'Of Per-Mafdet I assume?'

'Yes, and this is Neferure, a good friend of mine.' Khakhati bade her no more than a quick glance as Ahmes continued. 'We both welcome you to Thebes and to Karnak.'

Khakhati waited in silence. It seemed as though he expected something of them. He looked up at the temple and then glanced through the entranceway.

'If you wish, we may take you on a tour of Karnak.' Ahmes said.

'As I had hoped.'

Neferure and Ahmes exchanged quizzical looks before leading the way.

They passed through the pylon and into the temple courtyard. The morning sun warmed the stone beneath their feet, yet their paws, mostly insensitive to temperature, felt only the polished texture of the sacred ground.

The temple courtyard was completely open to the sky. Khakhati walked around the perimeter, looking at all the walls and columns. For a long while, no one said a word. Karnak spoke for itself.

The temple complex was as a great tapestry of history. Brightly painted figures, trapped in time, were carved upon every inch of wall and column. The layout of the temple symbolized the most ancient of events: the beginning of life. The temple stood as a stone version of the mound of creation rising out of the chaotic and primeval waters of Nun. The floor was highest at the inner sanctum of Amun-Ra, the mound upon which the sun god's golden statue stood.

'Do you know the story of how Per-Maahes was founded?' Ahmes eventually asked Khakhati, breaking the silence.

'Of course.' Khakhati fanned out his whiskers. Clearly

he was proud to tell the tale of his history and wasted no time in beginning the story.

'His name was Ibenre and hers was Nakhti. Ibenre lived beside a human of great importance: Tjaneni, the royal scribe and military general who served under Pharaoh Thutmose III.

'One day news came that the King of Kadesh, in the north, had allied himself with the armies of many other princes and kings. They intended to invade Egypt.

'Plans for war came as swiftly as the news bearing it. Turmoil swept about as the forces amassed. Ibenre watched Egypt's small and inexperienced army march towards foreign lands.

'There had been no wars during Hatshepsut's reign, prior to Thutmose's. Egypt was ill-prepared to face such a massive gathering of military might. Ibenre was no fool, and he saw this fact clearly.

'As other cats in the land hid and spoke of their fear and their fright, Ibenre—who knew little of those emotions—sought instead to bring the aid and power of Maahes to Thutmose's army. He travelled down the Nile towards Leontopolis, the city of lions, wherein lay Maahes's largest temple. At Giza Ibenre stopped for further directions. It was there, in the shadow of the great pyramid, that he met Nakhti.

'As a young kitten, Nakhti had lived at the house of a simple farmer in the Siwa Oasis. One fateful day, her mother was poisoned by the deadly fangs of a cobra. When the vultures came they spoke of strange lands to the east, bustling cities and a great river flowing forever.

'Filled with despair and anguish, Nakhti left behind the green oasis she had loved. Nakhti wandered into the barren desert, in the direction of the rising–sun, to the lands of which the vultures had spoken.

'To survive, she became fierce and strong, with a wilful spirit that burned stronger than the desert heat. She helped Ibenre find his way to Leontopolis, just as she would soon navigate him through the deserts and plains toward his destiny.

'Music and song filled the courtyard of Maahes's grand temple for the sole enjoyment of the sacred lions. As the grand cats savoured their prime cuts of meat, Ibenre sneaked towards the inner sanctum. He challenged a lion who refused him passage. Ibenre looked the giant cat in the eyes and declared that although he himself was not a lion, he had the heart of ten.

'Out of respect for Ibenre's intrepid nature, the lion relinquished his guard and granted the opportunity to speak with Maahes.

'Ibenre entered the inner sanctum and came upon a small golden statue of the great leonine god of war lit by raging torches. The music from the courtyard and halls had vanished.

'With a booming voice stronger than thunder, Maahes answered Ibenre's request to protect Thutmose and his army.

'You will bear my power with you on your quest,' Maahes said. 'If you follow Thutmose's army along their path, I shall bestow each of his soldiers the strength, grace, and power of a lion.

'If you succeed, and prove to be worth all that you claim, my powers will never leave you. They will flow through your veins until your blood turns to dust. You and your chosen descendants can bear my name in the title of your lineage evermore and speak with me wherever you please, even beyond the walls of this sanctuary.

'Ibenre accepted the challenge. He and Nakhti followed the Egyptian army along their route to the site of their undecided fate—before the fortress of Megiddo. They watched as Thutmose cunningly and bravely led his army single-file through the dangerous mountain pass of Aruna. He surprised the enemy armies, which had their backs turned to face the two easier paths around the mountain.

'Empowered by Maahes, the Egyptian chariots and spears fell upon the enemy with the strength and courage of a lion. Ibenre and Nakhti looked upon the battle with proud eyes as Thutmose commanded his army to victory.

'Much later, when all had returned to Egyptian soil, Horus spoke directly to Thutmose and told him of Ibenre's quest and the new lineage of Per-Maahes. Tjaneni then scribed the story of the war, in much greater detail than I have told you today, and it was inscribed upon the most inner walls of Karnak.'

'Ibenre,' Khakhati continued, 'was the strongest, bravest, and most cunning cat to ever live in Egypt. Only the strongest and bravest cats have been chosen to uphold the lineage. No cat of Per-Maahes has fully lived up to Ibenre's name, but likewise none has disgraced their title. My grandfather was a great fighter, brave and noble, but kept more towards the path of wisdom and knowledge. He died several years ago. My older brother took up our grandfather's watch guarding Pharaoh Seti's temple at Abydos. My mother resides in Memphis, in sight of the great pyramids. I heard there were no cats of Per-Maahes here in Thebes, so I decided to make a pilgrimage. Troubled times are upon us, and it's my duty to do what I can to protect the cats of Egypt.'

Pride was engraved on Khakhati's young face. Neferure and Ahmes continued their tour in silence.

The cats passed through the courtyard, the sun warming their short fur. Soon they came upon the next pylon, which separated the courtyard from the great hypostyle hall. They paused before the portal.

Neferure tested the air with her whiskers. 'No one but the priests, chantresses, and Pharaoh are allowed past this pylon ... at least as far as humans are concerned.' She then ventured into the darkness.

Khakhati gasped at the sight before his eyes, then quickly regained his proud demeanour. A forest of thick stone columns reached to the sky and supported a roof of painted stars. Clerestory windows filtered the sun, causing it to fall upon the ground as rays shining through a grand papyrus marsh. The floor was adorned with silver and polished to be as glossy as the surface of still waters. Nowhere could one turn without seeing gold glimmer in the darkness, for it was inlaid into every wall and column. The resplendence of the hall made all who walked through it feel as if the gods would soon be joining them.

One thing stood against the grandeur of Karnak.

An old and dishevelled cat slept by the far right wall. His

fur was dull and unkempt, his tail appeared to have been broken once at the base and never properly healed, and a tear was evident in his left ear, causing it to hang limply at the side of his head. He was enveloped in a deep sleep.

Khakhati walked past many rows of columns until he reached the wall. Ahmes and Neferure followed.

'Can someone explain this?' Khakhati asked.

'This is—' Neferure paused. 'Well, we don't really know who this is. He's been with the temple for as long as I can remember. We suspect he only ever moves to shake the dust off. Either that or the priests do the dusting for him. He used to speak occasionally, although he never said his name. Now he does little more than breathe. The most historic moment was the time he coughed up a hairball.'

Khakhati paced alongside the old cat. He sniffed at the air and studied the battered, sleeping lump on the ground. 'What happened to him?'

'Depends on whose story you go by.' Neferure said.

'How about his?' Khakhati asked.

'Those are usually the most interesting.'

'Are they the truest?'

'According to him.'

'Then let's start with the ear.'

'His ear was damaged in a battle with two cobras that were set upon him.' Ahmes said. 'Both snakes struck at the same time and from opposite sides. He moved quickly, barely evading their fangs. One of them caught his ear and tore through it. The snakes, he claimed, were moving too fast to stop themselves. Thus they struck and poisoned each other to death.'

Khakhati stared. 'What does everyone else say?'

'There are many stories,' Neferure replied. 'The most prevalent one is that he fell off a chair and it landed on him. The same holds true for the tail.'

'What does he maintain?' Khakhati asked with hesitation.

'He claims his tail was nearly bitten off as he escaped Anubis in the underworld.'

'During one of those casual visits, I suppose.' Khakhati thought for a moment. 'What does he eat?'

Neferure thought for a moment. 'Ahmes lays a mouse before him every day, and I believe some of the priests feed him. He always seems to find a way to consume his food when no one is around.'

'Why does he not want to speak with anyone?'

'We've stopped bothering to ask those questions,' Neferure said.

Khakhati lost interest in the old cat before him, and Ahmes resumed the tour. The three of them made their way through the shadowy columns and back to the main walkway. They continued along the east-west axis of the temple, directly in line with the sun's path through the sky.

When they finally passed through the third pylon, they found themselves again in the open air. The bases of four towering obelisks stood on either side of their path. One pair was built by Thutmose I and the other by his grandson, Thutmose III.

Their obelisks towered high, but they were still overshadowed by those of Hatshepsut that stood just behind the fourth pylon. Each of the massive gateways grew smaller as they reached the most sacred place in Karnak.

'Where we stand now was once the main entrance into the temple,' Neferure noted. 'Karnak is always growing.'

Khakhati tested the faint breeze with his whiskers and looked around, sniffing at the scent of fruit and incense in the air. He then looked to his right and noticed that the obelisk court was the crossroad between the two axes of the temple.

Neferure looked through the portal of the fourth pylon. 'Beyond that pylon,' she said, 'in the darkest and most secluded place of the temple, lies the inner sanctum of Amun-Ra. There his golden statue sits upon his solar barque. Only a select few ever set eyes upon it. No cat has yet done so. The seal is broken and the doors of the inner sanctum are opened only selectively during the day, starting at dawn, when the priests place food before the god, burn incense and sing hymns.'

The three of them peered into the darkness and saw flickering torchlight illuminate the raised inscriptions and images upon the stone. Khakhati seemed unwilling to venture further, so he turned to Ahmes.

'I have never heard the story of Per-Mafdet. Will you tell it?' he asked.

'I—' Ahmes's muscles tensed, and her ears scanned a noise only she could hear. Her claws pressed upon the polished stone floor, testing her footing. Instinctively her tail twitched.

Khakhati seemed to notice nothing. 'You do remember it, am I correct?'

Ahmes did not answer; instead she crouched low to the ground, her muscles gathering power. Seconds later a mouse appeared from behind a corner. All of Ahmes's senses were attuned to its movement. Neferure and Khakhati remained still. The mouse cautiously scurried closer, then froze and sniffed the air. Ahmes took one fluid leap and came down precisely upon her prey, killing it in seconds. Only when it lay lifeless upon the ground did she seem to remember where she was.

'What were you saying?' Khakhati stared at the dead mouse in awe. 'Do you know the story of how your lineage was founded?'

'Word for word from the scroll of Per-Mafdet.'

'Come,' Neferure said, 'tell it to us beside the sacred lake.'

Ahmes agreed. Khakhati's whiskers twitched with displeasure. *He probably assumes matters between cats of lineage are not meant to be discussed by common housecats,* Neferure thought.

They continued their journey southwards along the north-south axis of the temple. The whole of that axis was open to the sky. They passed the painted stone gateway and encountered two obelisks flanking the portal. Behind each of them stood a colossal red granite statue of Thutmose III, striding forward with his left foot.

Khakhati looked up at the statues. His eyes widened to absorb their power. Thutmose's legacy extended upon the walls. Intricate carved scenes depicted the exploits of one of Egypt's greatest warriors. Attached to the eastern wall was an alabaster sanctuary with a short stairway leading down into the courtyard containing the sacred lake.

'We must pass through there,' Ahmes said, glancing towards the sanctuary.

The sanctuary was small compared to many of the other structures at Karnak, and so the three cats reached the stairway at the end quickly. Sunlight washed the shadows of the columns towards the west. They sat down upon the top steps of the polished alabaster stairway, curling their tails against their bodies.

Khakhati looked around with wide-open eyes. Before him lay a vast rectangular pool stretching to the end of the long wall on their left. Geese swam upon the waters, as did many kinds of ducks. Palm trees grew along the edges of the sacred lake. The water was as green as the lotus leaves that grew upon the surface.

On the right hand side of the lake were the living quarters of the priests. They were built as rows of close quartered and quaint houses. Neferure's attention fixed on the newly reconstructed house that Sahu had once shared with Akhotep.

'This is the largest sacred lake in all of Egypt,' Ahmes noted. 'Soon the star Sopdet will rise and will bring about the Opening of the Year, a new beginning. It will be a day full of gold and music.' She turned to look at Khakhati. 'Karnak is home to many celebrations. Weeks from now you must also come to see the Opet Festival. Upon his solar barque Amun-Ra's emerges from the inner sanctum, carried upon the shoulders of priests. Then he sails across the lake before journeying the many steps to Luxor temple.'

Khakhati gazed across the sacred lake. 'I am indeed looking forward to the Opet Festival. I made sure to journey to Thebes before the Opening of the Year, for I wished to celebrate such a grand day in my new territory.'

'Only a few days to wait,' Neferure said. 'Yet I fear there will be little to celebrate.'

'Why do you say that?' Khakhati asked.

'A plague has hit the strays. By the time Sopdet rises, many housecats will also be ill and dying. The year will surely be off to a poor start.'

Khakhati stiffened his shoulders. 'Not if we keep the strays out of our territory.'

Neferure looked him in the eye. 'The plague is also spread by vermin.'

'That's fine.' Khakhati looked over at Ahmes. 'She will keep the vermin away from Thebes, and I shall defend us from the strays. I don't wish them ill, but the welfare of the housecats must come first.'

Neferure flattened her ears and looked at him in disbelief. 'The two of you cannot defend this city alone. What if either of you become ill? Surely, Khakhati, your amulet does not repel plagues.'

Khakhati tensed his muscles and narrowed his eyes. 'Then what do you propose we do?'

'We help cure them.'

'So it's impossible to defend against ill strays, but it is possible to cure them?' A hint of mockery infiltrated Khakhati's voice. 'Why do you care so much anyway?'

Neferure looked again toward the renovated house. 'Ahmes, you were to tell us the story of your lineage.'

Khakhati looked sideways at Neferure as Ahmes began her story.

'Before Per-Maahes was founded, but long after the establishment of Per-Sekhmet, there was a cat by the

name of Anheru. He lived and died during the reign of Hatshepsut. One night he had a dream as vivid as a waking hour. In that dream he saw the pharaoh disembark from her boat on her trading expedition to the land of Punt. Then the dream shifted and he saw a cobra strike, its deadly fangs rushing forwards. He believed so strongly in the truth of his dream that he hid inside a basket of goods and journeyed with Hatshepsut upon the Red Sea.

'Upon arrival in Punt he searched high and low for the snake, meeting with no success. He searched the baskets and the chests full of exotic goods destined for Egypt. He searched behind every rock and under every log near the areas to be passed over by Egyptian feet. Eventually he gave up. Anheru headed back to the boat and waited upon the deck, feeling foolish.

'The next day Anheru watched from the edge of the deck as Hatshepsut and her entourage returned with their goods and cages of exotic animals. Then he saw the snake behind a rock next to the boat, waiting upon her future path, coiled and ready to strike. As the pharaoh drew nearer, the snake felt her footsteps vibrate against the ground and drew up in anger. Anheru leapt straight down from the deck, and with unmatched precision landed upon the snake the instant it struck. He took its life before it could take Hatshepsut's.

'When she saw this display, Hatshepsut believed Anheru to have been sent from the goddess Mafdet herself. When they returned to Egypt, he lived out the rest of his life in the pharaoh's palace. He fell into favour with

Hatshepsut's own cat Nehebet, who was greatly esteemed for her skill hunting mice and rats.

'Hatshepsut was one day visited by Horus who told her to name Nehebet and Anheru as the founders of Per-Mafdet. However, one day Anheru was bitten and killed by a snake himself. The pharaoh decided that an usekh collar with a winged serpent would be given to all those of Per-Mafdet to protect them, and only the most skilled kittens would be designated by the cats to uphold the lineage.'

Khakhati's brow furrowed, and his eyes narrowed. 'You say you've memorized the story word for word from the scroll of Per-Mafdet?' he asked Ahmes.

'Yes, I have. What I told you was only a summary. The story on the scroll itself is much longer.'

'How were you able to read the texts?'

'I myself did not read them,' Ahmes replied. 'There's a cat living in Thebes who can decipher hieroglyphs. He found a copy of the texts and told me of it.'

Doubt grew on Khakhati's face. 'I wish to see this cat for myself. Whereabouts does he live?'

'His name is Heqaib, and he lives in a house in the scribes' district.' Ahmes perked her ears and leant forward. 'I can show you the way.'

'No,' Khakhati quickly responded. 'I must learn the layout of this city on my own now. If I need anything I'll search you out.'

Without acknowledging Neferure, Khakhati followed his own shadow through the sanctuary of Thutmose III and walked out of sight.

Ahmes sunk back onto her paws. 'What do you think of

him?' she asked when Khakhati was out of earshot.

'I think he's a little too obsessed with shiny objects.'

Ahmes looked at Neferure quizzically.

'I mean that he seems quite intent on setting a name for himself. No doubt he's very eager to live up to his heritage and prove himself worthy of his amulet and title.'

They gazed across the lake and watched the temple priests go about their daily routines. Birds floated upon the water surface, sending ripples from their wake. The summer heat shot through the air like an arrow of fire.

A scarab carefully rolled a pile of dung into a ball to protect her eggs, taking her time, as if it was the only thing in the world that really mattered. Soon new life, her young, would spring forth from apparent nothingness, just as Amun-Ra's rebirth at every dawn. Looking at the northeastern end of the lake, Neferure pictured the carved scarab that sat there. It was the statue of Khepri, god of life, renewal and sunrise. Ahmes looked at the sun. 'Well,' she said, readying to leave, 'time is mice.'

'Wait.' Neferure took one last look at the rebuilt house. 'Why don't we see what's taking place at the palace tonight?'

CHAPTER 4

At Court

THE GRAND HALL was thick with the smell of incense and the sound of drums. A steady rhythm pulsed through the ground. Guests mingled in a sea of fine linen and jewels. Men wore pleated kilts, and women wore white sheaths, their arms and necks dripping with gold. Many women wore elaborate wigs with perfumed wax cones on top. Throughout the night the heat of their bodies would melt the scent of lotus blossoms into their long black wigs.

Ahmes scanned the busy room for any signs of vermin or snakes.

Neferure looked at her. 'Seriously?'

'You never know.'

They sat and watched the proceedings. A pair of female dancers entertained a small crowd. Onlookers chanted, clapped, and lent the sound of cymbals to the air to encourage the dancers. Their arms were extensions of the string notes of the lyre, their hips guided by the deep drums. Delicate feet pivoted lightly upon the smooth tiled floor. Bathed in music, their movements were silent and graceful as lotus buds unfurling at dawn. Wearing only jewelled belts for clothes, their bodies glistened in the torchlight. Firelight weaved over and around their toned muscles as they undulated to the rhythm.

A blur of gold and stones and fur flew past Neferure and into the crowd.

Feet parted amid gasps. Wine spilled and splattered on the floor. Neferure glanced at Ahmes, then bolted toward the disturbance.

Khakhati tore through the room, eyes and ears on full alert. His ear swivelled backwards. He knew Neferure was pursuing him. He stopped next to the thrones and spun around.

'Mehen. Have you seen him?'

Stunned, Neferure searched her recent memory.

Khakhati drew forward. 'Have you seen him? Have you caught the scent of a stray?'

Puzzled, Neferure did not answer swiftly enough for Khakhati. He let out a low growl and disappeared into the crowd.

Ahmes met up with Neferure. 'What was that all about?'

'Mehen.' Collecting herself, Neferure sat down and gathered her tail around her body. 'I gather he has been spotted. We best be careful.'

Ahmes looked with concern to the pharaoh, seated among the congregation of royals.

Neferure suppressed a laugh. 'Do you really think a stray will assassinate the pharaoh?'

Ahmes shifted her paws. 'You never know.'

Ramesses, seated on his dais, watched the entranceway of the hall. Takhaet was seated near him, demanding the attention of Iset Ta-Hemdjert, the chief royal wife of the pharaoh. The High-Queen was of Asiatic origin, a marriage arranged to keep the peace between allied nations. Iset remained seated and watched as Ramesses stood up and joined with a group of his magistrates and Ta, the vizier of Upper Egypt.

Not long after, one of Ramesses retinue leant toward the pharaoh's ear. 'My Lord, Queen Tiye has arrived.'

With a wave of Ramesses' hand the drums halted and the dancers stood still. The crowd parted. All eyes turned to the woman entering the hall. Each elegant step of her small sandalled feet deepened the hush in the room. White linen slid like water over her curves. She was the calm centre of an electric storm of desire that swept through the court.

Tiye stopped and bowed before Ramesses. The pharaoh inclined his head and smiled.

Ramesses turned to the crowd, drawing his wife with him. 'Tonight we host a party in celebration of Queen Tiye's return.' The guests clapped and cheered. His hand found hers and gripped it tightly. 'I have invited the famed harpist Bentreshyt to play in her honour. Now, be seated and enjoy the wealth of food and music bestowed to us by Ra.' With another wave of his hand, the elegant melody of the harp glided into the air.

Guests seated themselves at intimate tables and wide benches. Servants appeared with ornate plates filled with breads, cheeses, lentils, fresh vegetables, and fruits.

Neferure's mouth began to water once the meats were delivered. Fish, duck, goat, and beef all tantalized her nose.

Rich spices and fresh herbs were infused into the dishes. Honey and figs were unfortunately slathered onto the food as well. *Why do humans always feel the need to alter the taste of their kills?* Their tampering was never an improvement. Still, she made plans to steal some later on.

Tiye joined with the group of magistrates. Ta's eyes lit up upon her approach. The vizier bowed without ever taking his eyes off of the queen. 'All of Thebes is glad you have returned, my lady, to grace us with the beauty and light of Isis herself.'

With a smile, Tiye touched his arm lightly. 'And I am glad you've looked after my husband in my absence.' She glanced teasingly at Ramesses, then returned her eyes to Ta. 'I trust your wife Hatia is doing well.'

'Hatia is well. We have welcomed a new son.' Ta's face was blank. He searched for more words.

Ramesses broke the spell by placing his hand upon Tiye's far shoulder. He drew her away from the group of admirers. Neferure's ears caught their words, though the humans could not. 'My dear, you must stop enchanting the magistrates,' he said with a slight smirk upon his lips. 'It interferes too much with their work.'

Tiye leant closer. 'You are the morning and the evening star. Let them stand in reverie if it inspires them. These are troubled times, and to see beauty is but a harmless diversion.' Glancing back at Ta, she then caught the eye of Iset. A furrow formed between the high queen's brows. The high queen looked to her son, the heir to the throne and the man who would next be pharaoh. At that thought, her features relaxed.

A smile grew on Tiye's lips. She guided Ramesses's face down to her own and graced his forehead with a kiss. The pharaoh watched with a wistful smile as Tiye drifted away to take her place beside Iset.

———✿———

As the evening festivities wore on, incense cones melted further into the thick wigs of the noblewomen, sending notes of lotus blossoms into the air. Neferure and Ahmes had managed to procure a meal of fish and and goat, which they ate at the base of the dais. Takhaet had left long ago, carried home by Hatia as she returned to her newborn son.

Tiye languished upon her throne, watching the entertainment unfold. Ramesses picked halfheartedly at his food. His muscles held deep tension, and his gaze jumped around the room. He broke out of his restlessness, rose and motioned for Tiye to join him.

Neferure and Ahmes exchanged glances as Ramesses and Tiye moved to a room away from the noise of the festivities. The pharaoh's guards blocked access for all humans. Cats, however, could go wherever they wished, and thus they sauntered through the legs of the guards and out onto the balcony, where they could still see and hear the couple speak.

Tiye closed the space between her and Ramesses. 'My lord, I hear rumours that the workers steal from you. Their labour strike will rob us of a proper burial and afterlife.'

Ramesses tightened his jaw at the mention of the strike. 'Yes, I was informed of that some time ago.'

'Then is something else wrong?' Tiye asked. 'You have been distracted all night.'

'I have not yet consulted Khesef-hra about this, nor anyone else.' Ramesses sighed. 'I have looked to Amun-Ra for how to end these troubles.'

Tiye nodded at this, but Neferure noticed her delicate hand clench at the mention of the high priest's name. The motion reminded her of Takhaet retracting a paw in disdain at a passing beetle.

'My communication with the gods and animals has been clouded of late,' said Ramesses. 'I fear a great evil is threatening Egypt.' He paused and looked deep into her eyes. 'I trust you will not share this with anyone.'

Neferure turned to Ahmes, their ears being the only ones other than Tiye's to hear the pharaoh's troubling news. 'A representative of the gods unable to commune with them. Has this ever happened before?'

Ahmes tilted her head. 'Not that I am aware of.'

Tiye rested her head on Ramesses's chest and embraced him gently. His shoulders slackened.

Ramesses ran his hand through her hair. 'Ta does not lie about the light of Isis shining within you.'

Tiye drew back. 'I heard rumours through Kesi, my handmaiden. May I call her? Her information may be of use to us.'

A guard gestured to the waiting Kesi, who walked into the alcove and knelt in front of Ramesses. Neferure sniffed the air Kesi's feet passed; she detected a faint scent of ashes.

Standing firm, Tiye looked straight into her handmaiden's eyes. 'Kesi, tell us what you've heard.'

'Forgive me, my lady. I do not dare repeat the gossip.'

'Tell us,' Ramesses insisted.

With a deep breath, Kesi continued. 'My uncle is an architect working on the tombs in the West Bank. In his letters he wrote that those who deliver the rations blame the pharaoh for the food shortages. They believe you have allowed the light of Ra to leave these lands, and that Egypt has fallen from favour of the gods.'

Ramesses narrowed his eyes.

Kesi added, 'Of course, I do not believe this, since our pharaoh has defeated both the Sea Peoples and the Libyan invasion.' She waited in stiff silence. 'May I leave now, my Lady?'

'Yes, Kesi.' Tiye looked to Ramesses for support, then glanced at her handmaiden. 'You've been brave and truthful. Ma'at will favour you.'

The handmaiden swiftly exited back into the grand hall. With her left the faint smell of ash.

Neferure turned to Ahmes. 'Do—'

Her eyes tracked movement in the garden. A large and stealthy cat skimmed the ground and vanished under a bush. His fur was brushed with copper. She had not seen him before, yet his apparence sparked a recollection. Something felt amiss.

In a moment of clarity her mind made the connections. 'Mehen! Send word to Khakhati.'

Neferure flew off the balcony in pursuit.

CHAPTER 5

Servants in High Places

LIKE A SHADOW through water Mehen slinked around corners and behind bushes so quickly that he almost seemed a ghost. Neferure chased him into the scribe's district, yet lost sight of him. Defeated, she rested awhile outside some houses, considering what motivation a stray like Mehen could have to enter the inner city.

Softly glowing oil lamps waved their flames in the windows of houses. One by one the lights were blown out, and the windows went dark. The night was hot and many people chose to sleep on their roofs, under the stars.

Neferure preferred the night. Upon waking, she saw stars shining in the darkened sky, their radiance mingling with that of the full moon low on the horizon.

A stillness daylight could never bring lay over the city. Dogs slept and people left the streets. No more hurrying here and there. No more shouts and arguments. Night belonged to the cats. Their highly attuned senses rested from the turmoil of living among humans.

In time all but one oil lamp was extinguished. Two children whispered faintly near the lamp, but Neferure's sharp ears caught every word. They were playing a game of senet. Pieces clacked and sticks were tossed upon the ground.

A man's silhouette moved across their window, heading north towards the outer city. He moved stealthily, glancing up and down the streets. Looking into the distance made him miss a strewn toy beneath his feet. He stumbled upon it and cursed. Inside the house the children froze.

'Did you hear that? I thought I saw something move,' one said.

'I told you father would hear us. You're being too loud,' the other replied.

'No. The noise was coming from outside.'

The man stopped, paused, then shrank into the shadows at the side of the house. Moments later he peered out from behind the corner. The light of the fire illuminated his face and cast deep shadows upon his features. It was none other than Qetu, the vizier of Lower Egypt.

Within seconds, the vizier had vanished into the darkness, his shadow creeping through patches of moonlight. Neferure followed him towards the north. To her ears Qetu's footsteps pounded as heavy as a bull, making him easy to track and to follow from a distance. Often the vizier stopped and glanced about. Yet just as he had missed the toy beneath his feet, he now missed the cat tracking his every step.

The buildings looked shabbier and the streets more unkempt as they travelled towards the edge of the city. Qetu turned west and then headed even farther until all that lay before his path was an abandoned one story house on the edge of a marsh.

Both hinges of the door were broken, and it was propped

up at an angle against the wall. Fallen plaster revealed the mud brick structure beneath. Flames of oil lamps danced through the gaps in the door. The shape of a cat carrying what looked like a serpent figurine passed by and disappeared into the darkness. The shape vanished too quickly for Neferure to identify by sight or scent.

Qetu gave the door one sharp knock, waited a second, then knocked twice quickly. A woman pushed the door aside. She moved and spoke like a serpent, her voice harsh and direct. Neferure remembered her from the boat that morning and from court. She was the handmaiden named Kesi.

'Again you're late.' Kesi squinted her eyes. 'If I had my way, this house would be the grand tomb that you seek.'

'There were complications. Our leader did not want to risk being caught. Not when we are so close to completing our plans. Instead he gave me a message and some instructions.'

Kesi waved a hand of dismissal. 'Soon we won't have to deal with these hassles. Know that if you displease me, Qetu, I will have my queen make your life miserable. For now you should come in before somebody sees you.'

Qetu entered the house and propped the door up behind him. Neferure poked her head through the gap at the bottom. No one noticed her watching eyes.

The house contained only a single room, and everyone inside could be easily seen. Packed dirt made up the floor, and wooden boxes were stacked in the far corner. A few people sat upon rickety old chairs, others upon the ground. Some Neferure recognized as nobles.

Why were these people meeting in secrecy?

Once everyone was settled, Qetu stood before his audience.

'He is known as the Enemy of Ra, The World Encircler, and the Serpent of Rebirth. Not since the end of the Old Kingdom has his cult risen. We are standing now upon a mountain of possibilities that Apep has opened up for us.'

Neferure gasped. They were speaking of the great and terrible serpent god of chaos and disorder who battled Ra every night as he passed through the underworld, trying always to swallow up his solar barque.

'We must thank Apep for giving us the power to rise to the positions we have.' Qetu looked around, making sure he had everyone's complete attention before continuing. 'Without him we would be but servants to our masters. Our new master will give back more than he takes. He only needs to rise to his full power and usurp Ra's position. For this he requires our complete allegiance. Long have we followed his ways, but now is the turning point. From here you either take an oath to follow him into the new age, or you slip into the background and rest forever in the safety of an ordinary life. This is where those truly loyal to Apep will show themselves by taking a lifetime oath, pledging their support and their lives. Nothing less than complete obedience and devotion will be tolerated, lest your family and lineage be destroyed.'

A war in the realm of gods, Neferure thought. *How could mortals plan to help? What could the Followers of Apep do that he himself could not?* She hoped that, through observing them, some further answers would come.

Qetu made his way towards the stack of wooden boxes. He opened the lid of the one on top and removed a serpent carved entirely of hematite. Its eyes were wrought of iron and bordered in gold, and the scales were inlaid with green malachite. A solar disc carved of garnet was being swallowed by the serpent's mouth. Qetu's muscles strained under the weight of the statue. 'I have called this meeting so that you may now pledge your allegiance to Apep.'

Neferure watched in bewildered silence as one by one the Followers of Apep walked up to the statue, placed their hands upon the stone and swore allegiance to the enemy of Amun-Ra. With each oath taken the air grew thicker, as if they stood inside a thundercloud. The statue seemed to grow in size and take on a life of its own.

One man hesitated before placing his hand upon the stone. 'What of the plague? Is that not of Apep's doing?'

'Do not fret over Egypt,' Qetu reassured him. 'This land will soon be ever more powerful, and so will you. The disorder of things will only be temporary until our Lord comes to power. Apep promises all will be remade better than in the past.'

Cautiously the man drew his hand towards the stone, as if expecting it to come alive and poison him. He then swore his oath and took his seat again upon the packed dirt.

When everyone was seated, Kesi spoke. She looked at Qetu through slanted eyes. 'The old priest—has his secret been buried with him?'

'I made sure of it. No one else knows what he knew. Everything is in order.'

'Now we just need the word,' another Follower said.

Kesi smiled. 'If only Ramesses knew what went on in this city. Now that we've all sworn our oaths, you must tell us where the temple is. When the time comes we will want to see our god rise.'

'Very well.' Qetu drew a deep breath. 'If one traces the path of—'

'Look!' someone shouted. 'A cat watches us from the door.'

Sharply Qetu averted his glance to the doorway. 'Someone chase it away,' he yelled.

'Why bother? It's a mere animal,' said one woman. 'I already chased one away before you came.'

Neferure fought the urge to run. Curiosity compelled her to stay until the last possible moment.

Kesi glared at the woman. 'Is Apep a mere serpent? Do servants of his never crawl upon this earth? That cat could be a manifestation of Bast herself. Until our god comes to power, you must be wary of everything, even the animals. They understand more than you realize. I can speak with their kind and enlisted the aid of one.'

Qetu cursed under his breath and ran after Neferure, but she was gone before he could shove open the door. The heavy wood crashed to the ground, and its sound echoed through the streets. She ran hard towards the marshlands bordering the Nile. Qetu picked up a stone and hurled it into the night. Air rushed past Neferure's leg as the stone slammed into the ground. Another stone flew through the air and landed before her path.

The ground beneath her gave way, and she lost her footing. Neferure disappeared into the void below.

She fell down a waterfall of sand and landed upon hard

ground. For a short while she lay still, listening for Qetu's footsteps, hearing only the sand grains settling. Neferure got up and shook her fur clean.

Takhaet's words sounded in her head. *Curiosity will be the death of you.* Perhaps it would, but now she had uncovered things she could not leave secret. What knowledge did Akhotep take with him to the grave? If everything was prepared, why were The Followers still waiting for Apep's word? Something still held them back. Why anyone would follow an evil deity was beyond Neferure's understanding, and she preferred to keep it that way.

Their leader must be someone important for him not to risk being seen, perhaps someone even closer to Ramesses than Qetu. Khesef-hra was surely not a suspect, for as the high priest he had power nearly akin to the pharaoh. She dared not think that their leader was one of Ramesses' sons, or Ta, the vizier of Upper Egypt. Little time did she spend inside her own home, and so she did not know much of Ta's comings and goings. Takhaet, on the other hand, would know. Never did she think a day would come when her sister could prove useful.

She looked around the cavern and fanned her whiskers outward to test the air current. The walls were of rough rock and packed dirt. Parts of the roof had caved in, leaving rubble and dust beneath rays of the moon. Someone spoke from beyond the darkness.

'Neferure?'

The voice sounded very familiar—impossibly familiar. It called her back through time, layered with memories she had tried to abandon.

A pair of emerald green eyes emerged from the shadows. The darkness washed away under the moonlight as a cat stepped out to greet her. This was surely an illusion.

'Sahu?'

CHAPTER 6

The Promise

NEFERURE'S HEART QUICKENED. The sight of Sahu brought strong, desperate relief that shattered all thoughts and concerns. She did not wait for an explanation, but rushed to greet him, dodging fallen rocks upon the ground.

Sahu backed away. 'You can't take my scent back to the inner city.' He looked to the ground. 'If anyone knows I'm alive, they'll kill me.'

Neferure shrunk back onto her paws. 'What do you mean?' She perked her ears forward and tilted her head to the side.

Sahu looked to his left. There the cavern opened to the marsh. Ripples ran through the water and reflected moonlight played upon the cavern roof above.

'They will kill me,' he said, still avoiding Neferure's gaze, 'simply because my being alive means I have betrayed Akhotep. As a temple cat it was my duty to protect Karnak and its inhabitants from evils seen and unseen by human eyes. Instead I ran.'

'You could have been running for help.'

'Cats in other houses woke their humans when the fire

started. I did not wake Akhotep.' Sahu's glance fell to the ground. 'I wasn't sure I had time to wake him. The fire spread unusually quickly. Neferure, when I saw it, I knew I could either save my life or die with him. So I grabbed a scroll he had been reading and left, hoping it was of some importance. The other cats will not see it as I do. I doubt anyone but you will.'

Sahu's eyes glazed over as he remembered that fateful night, indifferent to the time that had passed. 'I heard screams, shouts of fear that the temple would burn as I ran into the night. I could not make my way back into the inner city, and no one would help me. There was no way I could get to you.'

Neferure studied Sahu's downcast bearing—a mirror to his frame of mind. Clearly he had not yet forgiven himself, although he always stood by his choices with conviction. Sahu had forsworn his duty as a temple cat to avoid dying a needless death. Had he also forsworn the promise he made to always be there for her? Some promises were kept deeper in the heart than others, but Neferure could not help but doubt him. If he could break one oath, why not another?

Even worse, if Sahu himself doubted his actions, he could never pass the weighing of the heart ceremony and enter Amenti whenever he did die.

Neferure shied away from her misgivings and changed the subject. 'Why do the strays not use this space?'

'They say it is cursed. That whoever enters this cavern will soon face hardship or death. I find that hard to believe. Such tales are rarely created from reason.'

Neferure made her way to where the marsh met with

the cavern and sat down, watching the slow current weave around a thin log resting in the mud.

Sahu stepped forward a few paces. 'I tried to seek a better life for myself,' he said, breaking the silence. 'For a while I thought I'd found it. I had a home, I finally had peace, and I had you. Perhaps those things were never meant for strays. Nevertheless, there was one thing I was not prepared to give up.' His glance met with hers.

'I would find that touching…' Neferure turned her head away.

'What is it?'

She continued, all the while studying the moonlight dance upon the marsh. 'You aren't going to pass the trials of Amenti any easier than you could walk right into the centre of this city. You will not pass the weighing of the heart ceremony.'

Sahu's response came quick. 'Neferure, do not fear the great scale. The flame of our hearts shall burn just as strongly in the stars as they do on earth, and they will do so together.'

They faced eye to eye. 'How can you be sure?' Neferure asked. Sahu did not reply. Paying closer attention to his appearance, Neferure noticed his poorly groomed fur and discovered a fresh wound on his back, hidden under his silver coat. 'What happened to you?'

Sahu studied the mud caked into his paws. 'There are certain hardships that come along with being reaccepted by strays.'

'Did you succeed?' Neferure was sure of what his answer would be.

Now self-conscious about his appearance, Sahu began licking his paws and grooming his face. 'No. They couldn't care less about my current standing among housecats. However, they don't take it well when someone deserts their kind for what they call "a comfortable and useless life".'

Neferure was finding the whole discussion surreal, an illusory conversation with a ghost rather than a living being. 'Is that what they think about housecats?' She cared little for what strays thought of her kind but wanted to keep the conversation moving.

'The strays believe they're responsible for keeping the housecats alive and free from snakes or scorpions that would otherwise enter the city,' Sahu said. 'In their minds, they're the sole protectors of Thebes.'

'Surely they must allow housecats who have become strays into their territory,'

'Occasionally, but not without hardship. Usually you have only one chance to earn their acceptance.'

'The strays pose other dangers now.'

'The plague. I know,' Sahu said in passing, as if it held no threat to him. 'I've seen it firsthand. Their leader, Mehen, has not been affected himself, but he's having a hard time keeping the rest of the strays under control. Some go mad before they become ill. It certainly makes them dangerous.'

Neferure fought the urge to brush against Sahu and comfort him. She wondered how the past forty days had been for him. He'd fallen as far as one could. 'Just this morning a cat of Per-Maahes arrived.'

'I know,' Sahu said. 'He made sure his presence was known. The strays do not approve of him.'

'I must tell you something.' Neferure took a deep breath. 'Akhotep died at the hands of some cult of Apep. I am sure of it, as I spied on a meeting of theirs. He knew of something, a secret he took with him to the grave. This secret might be connected to the scroll you spoke of.'

Sahu perked his ears. 'I hid the scroll under the roots of a shrub outside Heqaib's house before I left the city, hoping he might find it and translate it.' He moved to sit at the edge of the marsh, his paws nearly touching the water. 'I had a feeling Akhotep's death was not accidental. I stumbled upon that cult after being chased from stray territory. I tried to spy on them earlier tonight and heard a bit about the serpent called Apep, but I was chased away before I could find out more.'

'This must be why Akhotep was so worried in his final days. He knew his life was in danger.'

'The vizier Qetu is one of the Followers, and so is the handmaiden Kesi,' Neferure added. 'He mentioned that they enlisted the aid of a cat. Queen Tiye's handmaiden claims she can hear us speak.' A memory flooded to the surface of her mind. 'Before I spied on them, I saw a cat slip by, carrying the figurine of a serpent. I could not tell who it was.'

Sahu retold his own experience. 'Before I was chased away, I saw the Followers hand the figure to the cat you speak of. I did not look through the door out of fear they would discover me. Instead I tried peeking through the window of the house, but a stack of boxes blocked my sight. I could see little more than shadows moving on the wall and the flickers of oil lamps. It looked to me as though the cat was wearing an amulet, although I could be mistaken.'

A group of fish caught Sahu's attention as they swam close to the dry land. With the keen eyes of a skilled hunter, he watched and waited for his opportunity, continuing in a stilted and preoccupied speech. 'If you could have Heqaib translate the texts it may bring us closer to understanding Akhotep's secret.' In a flash his silver fur struck the water's surface and his black claws pierced smoothly through the scales of a fish. Sahu flipped his dinner onto the ground before him, paused, and then looked up. 'Akhotep was the only human who ever cared about me. I would like to give his death meaning.'

'I was trying to do the same for you. That's what brought me here.' An awkward silence hung in the air. Neferure shifted her paws. 'I'm sure Heqaib will be more than glad to do the translating.' She looked down at his fish, wishing she could share the catch but knowing there was plenty of food for her back at her own home.

Sahu's posture righted and his ears drew forward. 'In the meantime I will do what I can to get information about the Followers themselves and how they plan to help Apep defeat Amun-Ra. As long as they don't travel too far into the inner city, I should be fine.'

'While Heqaib works on the translation, I'll search out the leader of the cult. I suspect it is one of Ramesses's sons, or perhaps Ta.' Neferure felt troubled at the thought of a traitor in her own household. 'I'll also look for more clues about Akhotep's secret.'

'Remember,' Sahu said, 'someone among our kind does not have our best interests at heart. We don't yet know who is working for the Followers. Until we do, it would be best to keep what we know to ourselves.'

Neferure looked again at the wound on Sahu's leg and at his underfed appearance. His actions were brave, but she wasn't sure they were very wise. 'I still don't understand why you had to do this.'

Sahu turned and looked her in the eyes.

'All my life I've never known much of a past, but you've given me a future. I'm not about to let that future fly away as the sands of the desert. Terrible things are about to happen, and I won't watch them take their toll on you from my seat among the stars because I took the safe route out of this world. Remember, I promised I would always be there for you, that I would never let anything bad happen to you so long as it was in my power to prevent it. I may have dishonoured a servant of the gods, but I haven't yet broken my promise to you. If my actions are judged against me, then so be it.' He straightened his posture, and his eyes revealed a soul filled with more resolve and devotion than ever before.

The immensity of his promise dawned on Neferure, who realized she had not given anything in return. 'Then let me make a promise of my own. No matter what happens or what I have to do, I will see to it that your heart passes the weighing ceremony. Even if I have to give my own in place of it.'

They looked at each other. The distance between them seemed to grow again at this new separation. Sahu was alive, but Neferure knew she might never find peace at his side, even in death.

'I shall meet you again in two days.' Neferure leapt onto a thin log protruding from the marsh and dug her sharp claws into the damp bark. Stabilizing herself with her tail, she scaled back towards dry land. She paused once to look back at Sahu, half expecting to see only rocks and air.

CHAPTER 7

Ancient Texts

KARNAK TEMPLE STOOD strong before Neferure's path, its long flags dancing delicately in the soft morning breeze. She drew closer to the temple as she made her way back into the city. The sky above was lit like an ocean of crimson flames, and the first light of the sun shone as a torch upon the water, flickering with the passing current. Once again the gold tipped obelisks were ablaze. Never could Neferure imagine a time when only barren land had laid in place of Karnak. It seemed as much a part of Egypt as the Nile.

She retraced her path. She had never been so far from home and did not know what dangers lurked down those streets. People were waking up, readying for another day's work. Neferure watched them hurry around and felt glad her own life was not so regimented. Few cats could understand the concept of surrendering one's personal freedom to suit another's will. She certainly was not one of those few.

In contrast to the adventure of the night before, life again followed the same rhythm it had for centuries. She waited to be woken from her surreal dream back into a world where the strange events she witnessed had not taken place. Had she really stumbled upon a secret cult of Apep? Did she truly see Sahu, or had he been a ghost? Her memories seemed both vivid and clouded, as if for a brief moment Isis had lifted the veil cast between worlds. Even though her mind could not grasp recent events, the eyes of her heart knew it had all been real.

A sharp yowl pierced the air.

Neferure paused. Her whiskers tested the air currents while her ears and eyes scanned for any sign of danger.

'Chase them out of the city!' came a yell from the closest cross street. Moments later a group of cats, led by Khakhati, appeared. They were fending off strays and attempting to drive them back into their own territory beyond the borders of the city. 'Do not get bitten by them!' he yelled. 'That is how the plague spreads.'

As Neferure watched the battle draw past her, it became clear something was very wrong with the strays' behaviour. A few clawed and bit viciously at the air, whether or not anyone was in front of them. Their pupils were dilated despite the brightness of the sun. Others had greater mental control, which allowed their rage to be more directed, and thus lethal.

Khakhati swiped at the strays with his claws unsheathed, driving them further away from the city. At times he took on two of them at once, yet always remained on the offensive.

'This city is ours!' said one of the strays. Khakhati dealt a massive strike to his face, raking his claws across his opponent's jaw.

Another stray yelled, 'one of you must have set this plague upon us! Why are no housecats ill?'

Khakhati wrinkled his nose and bared his teeth. 'Because our hearts are not wretched.'

Further enraged by Khakhati's words, one stray broke free from the battle and ran straight into the inner city towards Karnak. His legs trembled under his weight when his uncoordinated paws hit the ground.

Without a thought, Neferure blocked his path. His eyes were wild with rage and anxiety. He attacked her without concern for his own life. His sight focused on Karnak, not on the battle before him.

Neferure had not fully prepared herself for a fight, and she quickly lost ground to her opponent's attack. She parried some blows and escaped others. In one swift stroke he leapt forward and bit down upon her left front leg. His mouth was full of frothy saliva that mixed with drops of hot blood running down her golden fur. Pain pulsed in her wound, but she ignored the agony. Desperately she continued fighting to keep the ill stray from entering the city. Claws rushed at her face. Neferure turned sharply away, and in doing so she looked towards the sunrise.

Again she saw it. The stream of light poured across the sky and flowed through the land. Her vision of the world was obscured and her muscles could barely move. A powerful current of force swept around her as if she were struggling against a fast flowing river. Faintly she could see her attacker swiping anew with his paws. Time moved slowly, and adrenaline raced through her blood. The throbbing of her wound lessened. From the corner of her vision, she could see her attacker's claws unsheathing from his paw and edging again towards her head.

Khakhati was upon the stray before the paw could hit her. He bit the cat hard in the neck until he yowled in pain. Khakhati backed away.

The stray looked upon his opponent with clouded eyes as life drained from his body. He staggered away. Many paces later his legs gave way, and he crashed lifeless to the ground.

As the sun rose, the river of light got weaker; it faded from Neferure's view and released its hold over her. Pain pounded again in her leg. Gradually she regained her senses and hid her wounds from all, as it would be a death sentence for her as well. Sweat drenched the footpads on her paws. In shock she looked upon the fallen body. 'Why did you do this?' she said, turning to Khakhati.

'Better I kill him than the plague,' Khakhati said. 'In time more would have died had I not done so. You may have been one of them.'

Blood was splattered upon his amulet, yet he remained uninjured. Khakhati watched the other strays limp back towards their own territory. Some moaned in anger, others in pain. One halted his slow escape and looked at Khakhati. With his blood-drenched jaw he let out a low growl. 'Mehen will not enjoy hearing of this.'

Khakhati gave no reply. Instead he turned toward the cats who had helped him in the fight. 'Keep all strays away from our territory, and kill any who are ill and try to enter this city.'

Midday arrived by the time Neferure finished cleaning her wound and made her way to Heqaib's mud bricked house to deliver the texts. It took time for the shock of the stray's attack to wear off. For a few hours she had tried, in vain, to make sense of her unusual experiences with the river of light. Not only were those experiences confusing, but they were also dangerous. If Khakhati hadn't been there, would she have lost her life? Proudly she told herself she would not. In any case, she had not enjoyed losing control over a situation. Until she could figure out her predicament, she would avoid the outdoors during sunrise.

Soon she arrived before the familiar mud bricked house wherein lived a most unusual cat. She looked to the side. A row of three low-growing shrubs were rooted to the right of the doorway. They were old and dry, though their roots reached deep into the earth. In certain spots the sand and dirt had been blown or dug away, leaving crevices between and under the roots. Branches and leaves swept the ground, easily obscuring those hideaways from curious human eyes. Neferure felt certain the scroll would still be there.

She quickly discovered she was wrong.

Many possible answers raced through her head as she sat beneath the dry leaves. Would a human have looked in there? Did the scribe find it and take it away? Could it have been another cat? Perhaps Heqaib himself found it and was already reading through it.

Neferure found her gaze shifting into the distance. Her sight narrowed in on a mother walking hand in hand with her child. At first there seemed nothing noteworthy about them. The mother's hair was short and frazzled. A thick lock of braided black hair grew upon the child's other-wise bald head. He was a typical example of an Egyptian youth—only he had an ancient scroll clutched tightly in his left hand. His mother seemed not to care where or how he had acquired it. She paid no attention as the boy tapped it against his leg.

Neferure's eyes widened as she watched her answers walk away in the hands of that small child. Perhaps she could sneak underfoot and trip him up. That plan had worked often for her in the past. However, something disturbing had just finished raiding a nearby trash pile: a hunting dog.

His build was that of a supreme runner, long legged and lithe. On open ground Neferure stood no chance if he decided to continue the feud between their species. Cats were revered and pampered throughout the land, while dogs were utilitarian. The difference in treatment had cre-ated a divide where dogs, oxen, and donkeys were subspe-cies. Unlike donkeys and oxen, dogs were eternally bitter about their station in life.

Snapping back to reality, Neferure realized that height was her only hope. She looked about and noticed only a thin and young palm tree growing between her and the scroll.

The child stuck out his hand to greet the dog, who natu-rally responded with great exuberance and rushed over to lick the child's face. Giggles of laughter escaped into the air. The mother's face contorted in absolute shock as she watched her son's short life flash before her eyes. She let out a desperate yell for the dog to stay away. In the midst of the confusion, the child dropped the scroll from his hand.

It fell to the ground, instantly forgotten. Neferure waited, patient and prepared, for an opportunity to grab the scroll. She dared not brave triggering the dog's hunting instincts.

In what she supposed was an act of selfless bravery, the mother jumped towards the exhilarated dog, grasped her hand firmly around his leather collar and pulled him a safe distance away from her child. With his tongue hanging out of his mouth, the dog stood where he was placed, quizzically looking back and forth from mother to child, asking repeatedly what he had done wrong.

Afraid that the child would regain interest in the scroll, Neferure took that golden opportunity, with everyone distracted and the dog held back, to chance her retrieval of the texts. She dashed forward. The dog caught sight of her, and all former events were torn from his memory. He broke free from his restraint and raced after Neferure. She widened her gait and in one flawless dive swooped down upon the scroll. Barely grazing her jaw upon the ground, she seized the papyrus in her mouth. Her front paws grabbed at the earth, and she spun so sharply that dust rose in the air. She then sped off towards the safety of the palm tree. The dog came upon nothing but empty ground.

Neferure jumped onto the dry and rough bark of the palm tree, scaling up its trunk until she reached its crown of leaves. She looked at the ground and saw the dog directly beneath her, barking fervently.

The mother cradled her child in her arms, thanking Ra for his narrow escape from death. Nothing but giggles escaped the child's mouth as he watched the dog place his front paws against the tree trunk.

The thin young palm tree swayed back and forth precariously, bringing Neferure dangerously close to the dog. 'You are one of those housecats,' he said. 'Your life is forfeit.'

Neferure dug her claws deeper into the wood.

A deep human voice reached her sharp ears. It came from a group of scribes meandering their way down the street, talking about their jobs and their lives. Neferure recognized the voice of the scribe who lived in Heqaib's house.

'I swear I saw my cat trying to read hieroglyphs,' the scribe said as he looked around for anyone who may be listening. Upon seeing the woman and child nearby, he leant over, and in a hushed voice continued his story. 'He was seated in front of a new scroll I was working on, and his eyes moved slowly up and down the page. When he saw I was watching, he fell off the table, and ran.'

The dog jumped and snapped at Neferure each time the tree top swayed forward and came within his reach.

'You're lucky,' another scribe replied. 'The most exciting thing my cat ever does is cough up hairballs.'

Soon the dog learned that by applying more pressure to the tree with his front paws he could cause it to bounce back closer to him. Neferure greatly wished people would only selectively breed dumb dogs.

A third scribe chimed in. 'Give it a few years and that cat of yours will be designing and building pyramids.'

The tree arched backwards, seeking to brush the ground and gathering the energy to drive forward again. Neferure knew this time it would bring her close enough to the ground for the dog to reach her.

In recognition of the third scribe's voice, the frazzled woman turned around. 'Put your dog on a leash! He was biting my child!'

Air sailed past Neferure's face as the tree picked up momentum, rushing towards the ground and straight into the dog's eager jaws. The dog's muscles were coiled and quivering in anticipation.

'Ineni!'

Startled, the dog shrunk backwards. His ears pulled back, torn between obedience and the desire to maim his eternal enemy. Neferure hid her head, and the scroll, behind a large palm leaf so that no one would see what she held.

Ineni was dragged away by his master. The tree bounced backwards yet again with Neferure still clinging to it. His protestations just sounded like raspy barks to the humans. Once the tree became still and everyone had turned away, Neferure scaled down and skidded off towards Heqaib's house.

She pushed aside the old wooden door and was met with the scent of fresh papyrus. Several scrolls lay stacked upon a wooden table near the entranceway. Neferure searched all the rooms in the house, finding no one. As a last resort she climbed the stairway that lead to the rooftop. Heqaib was there, seated right at the edge, quite an unusual place for him. Unlike his other resting spots, it was out in the open and far from secret. She took a few steps forward and laid her scroll upon the ground.

'Don't draw attention. I think they're on to me. They're also making fun of my brother and his problem with hair-balls.' Heqaib glanced over his shoulders at the group of scribes down below. 'They know I can read their language.'

'Yes, they know,' Neferure said. 'That's why you'll need to keep this scroll extra secret. These are the texts Akhotep was reading before he died.'

Heqaib's bolted over to the scroll, unraveled it with his paws, and scrutinized it from top to bottom. The more he read the wider his eyes grew. 'How did you find this?'

'I'm not able to discuss that at the moment. I just need you to decipher it.' She looked up at Heqaib. 'Can you do that for me?'

'Of course I can.' He recoiled his head in offence. 'Do you know what this scroll is?'

Neferure took a glance at the antique papyrus. She had a strong suspicion as to its purpose but preferred to feign ignorance. 'A story with many green snakes?'

'This is the Book of Apep.' Heqaib's eyes beamed with fascination.

'So Akhotep did know...' Neferure whispered to herself.

Heqaib looked up. 'Did you say something?'

'No.' Neferure's eyes shifted. 'I just wanted to know what was special about the book of Apep.'

Heqaib raised his eyelids so wide that the tips of the whiskers above them nearly touched the tops of his ears. 'What's special about it? This scroll contains all the knowledge of spells and rites needed to defeat the enemy of Ra.' He looked back and forth between Neferure and the scroll. 'I would really like to know where you got this.'

'As soon as you decipher it, I'll let you know.'

Heqaib put his nose to the papyrus. 'It smells of smoke. Was it in the fire? I wonder how it could have survived.'

'I wouldn't know. Someone might have kept incense too close to the scroll.' Neferure didn't want to tell Heqaib about Sahu or the followers of Apep lest he give anything away to another cat. She figured he himself was trustworthy but could not be certain. Until she knew who was conspiring with the Followers, she decided to say little. 'Anyway, it's best that I move along and you begin your translations.'

Heqaib studied the length and complexity of the texts. 'I'll try to have it done by tomorrow.'

'Why tomorrow?' Neferure questioned. 'Why not today?'

'The scroll is quite long, and it will take me a while to decipher. This is a temple document, and unless you want it taken away, I'll need to keep it very secret.' Heqaib's voice quavered. Neferure looked him in the eye as she tried to figure out if he was telling the truth or trying to stall the deciphering process. Whoever was helping The Followers could have frightened or persuaded Heqaib to prevent any attempts to find out information against them.

Not knowing whom to trust was frustrating. Sahu had seen the shadow of a cat wearing an amulet. Khakhati and Ahmes were the only two cats in Thebes who wore amulets, and they both had recently spoken to Heqaib and knew of his talents. The only thing Neferure could do was personally ensure Heqaib kept on track.

'This evening I'll be back to see how much you've translated.' Neferure did not wait for Heqaib's agreement before slipping back down the stairs into the dimly lit house.

Neferure had nearly reached the door when she ran into Ahmes delivering a mouse to Heqaib. Her whiskers were fanned out on either side of her prey, testing for the slightest of movements to be sure it was dead.

Neferure's body ached and her mind was struggling to keep the tiredness at bay. 'I'll save you some trouble,' Neferure said, distracted. 'He's hiding on the roof.'

When Neferure returned to her home, she immediately searched out her sister. Unsurprisingly Takhaet was found seated on the lap of Hatia. The woman was stroking Takhaet's fur in an automatic fashion, her mind dwelling upon other matters. Pale golden fur flew up in the air with each hand stroke, a vexed look upon her sister's face.

Takhaet bit Hatia's hand, jumped off her lap, and turned around to glare at the woman. 'For the last time, don't pet me half-mindedly.'

Takhaet showed no care for how she'd hurt Hatia's feelings. The woman, not knowing what she did wrong, stood up and watched the two cats in bewildered silence.

Takhaet then turned to Neferure, ignoring Hatia. 'What have you been up to?' she asked as she started grooming her left shoulder. Takhaet scrutinized her sister's appearance. 'You look rather worn out.'

'I've just been exploring.' Neferure nonchalantly licked her paw. She realized her fur was scented with city's edge and promptly redirected the conversation. 'I was wondering if you've noticed any change in Ta's schedule.'

The vexed look returned to Takhaet's face. 'What would I care? It's not as if he ever feeds me. He only trips over me whenever he's drunk too much beer.' Her aggravation quickly turned into suspicion. 'Is this in some way helping you avenge Sahu's death? If it is then you're better off trying to catch that mouse who keeps eating out of my food dish.'

'No, this is not helping me *avenge* Sahu's death.'

'Good.' Takhaet turned to walk away. 'Strays deserve none of our help.'

Neferure shifted her thoughts to more pressing issues. What was Akhotep's secret? Was it somehow connected to the ancient scroll? Akhotep had never seemed to keep secrets. He had always freely given his thoughts and time, holding nothing to himself but the ankh he always wore around his neck. The fact that he would keep a secret now meant that it was truly dangerous.

Neferure's mind and body gave into exhaustion and so, whether Egypt was safe or not, she gave the matter no further thought. Walking to the border of the city and back, delivering a scroll to Heqaib, finding out Sahu was alive, having a mystical experience, escaping a homicidal dog, and battling with an ill stray had been enough adventure for one day. Neferure made her way over to her bed of linen in the far corner of the room and fell fast asleep.

CHAPTER 8

The Forbidden Temple

SAHU CREPT ALONG the edge of the marshland, keeping his paws upon dry ground whenever possible. The day was drawing to an end, and the sun cast a deep golden glow upon the land in prelude to its setting. Midday's great head had dissipated into the pleasant warmth of a summer evening.

A Nile sunbird perched upon the branches of a tall willow tree, his radiant yellow underbelly facing the light. Iridescent blue wing feathers glistened as the bird gave his voice to the wind, singing a song worthy to grace the ears of gods.

Above the open water a pied kingfisher dove into the cool river and snatched up a fish in his long beak. Far off into the distance, a hippopotamus twitched her ears as she slowly walked along the silty bottom of the Nile.

Sahu hid behind a curtain of reeds as he stalked through the marsh after Qetu. For a long while he tracked the vizier as the man searched through the marshes, looking for something specific.

Birds, frogs, fish and turtles all quickly made their escape as Qetu lumbered through the watery land. The Nile sunbird broke his beautiful melody to sound a warning cry as he fluttered deep into the reeds.

Concealed from view, Sahu watched Qetu search. What did he need to find if the Followers waited only for the word to be given?

A lone crocodile lounged near the bank of the marsh. Only part of his body was submerged under the water, as though he was making a half-hearted attempt to hide from his prey. He was completely absorbed in his own world, muttering to himself in a droning baritone voice about how terrible he was at being a predator.

'I'm sure I couldn't even eat that man over there if I tried,' the crocodile said, 'and he's not even suspecting anything. He's faster than I am, and humans fight too much. It's just no use. No use at all. I wonder what lily pads taste like?'

At first the crocodile's presence alarmed Sahu, though soon he became annoyed at the constant stream of down-hearted speech. In time he fell into his own thoughts, tuning out the voice of the crocodile and reminiscing upon the events that had brought him to that very place and time. Though he deeply loved Neferure, at times he could not understand her mind. Why had she been so distant upon learning he was still alive?

Sahu cared little about what the other cats thought of him. If there was a fault to his species, it was their unrelenting desire to save face and avoid humiliation. Such was not often the case with Sahu. It had taken him great courage to rise from his life as a stray to the esteemed position of a temple cat. He had stood alone most of his journey, looked down upon by many for challenging his heritage.

At first he had succeeded in his quest for a better life. He had even won the support of most housecats. Now he had fallen harder than ever. Sahu had spat in the face of his great privilege.

Although he could not blame the other cats for their views towards him, he did not find them valid. He would fight for what he believed to be right, even if no one else agreed with him or his choices. Unlike his past struggles, there could be no reward. Even if he were able to waylay The Follower's plans to bring Apep to power, he could not go back to either his life as a stray or as a temple cat. He was not sure what future he would have to share with Neferure, in this life or in the afterworld.

The crocodile caught sight of Sahu and attempted to look fearsome. With a yawning mouthful of misaligned teeth, he looked absurd instead. Sahu stared blankly as the creature continued his muttering. 'Oh, I'll never be able to keep up the code,' he said. 'I'm horrible at this opportunistic predator thing. It means I always have to look for the opportunities. I need time to find the meaning of life.'

He went on in that manner of speech for a good while. Sahu was about to offer himself as a free meal just to make the droning stop when at last he heard Qetu's voice. The vizier was muttering to himself under his breath.

> *'It is hidden in whence it all began,*
> *Over which the Nile long has ran.*
> *Still waters forever kept it clean,*
> *Resting on ground long unseen.*
> *Year upon year has always passed,*
> *Celebrations to which solar light was cast.'*

'Hmm,' Qetu muttered to himself, 'it has to be some-where beneath the Nile, below the flood plain level and somewhere the sun shines upon. Meaning it could be any-where. It might not even be in Thebes at all. How are we supposed to figure out this riddle in just a few days? We'll never find it in time.'

From behind the curtain of reeds, Sahu watched Qetu continue his search under logs and rocks for the object he couldn't find. The more the man searched, the more distressed he became. Behind him the Nile took its time, flowing slowly over roots and rocks on its long meandering route to the ocean.

What exactly are they trying to find? Sahu wondered. More questions and yet no answers.

A woman came walking through the marshland. Her white dress trailed over mud and water, and her sandals crushed any plant they trampled upon. She was careful not to be seen, yet confident in her stride. When she finally caught up with Qetu, she leaned over and spoke in a low voice. 'I wish to pay homage to our god. For that I must know where the temple is. I have not been able to meet with our leader as it would compromise our work. It's safe now to speak.'

Sahu's ears perked up. Neferure had not mentioned any-thing about a temple devoted to Apep. Had it slipped her mind or did she not know? In any case, it couldn't hurt to learn its whereabouts.

Hesitantly, the vizier heeded the woman's request. 'Yes Kesi, it lies in the northeastern desert. Follow the snake's tracks in the sand. Great winds may stir the sands beside the path, but the serpent tracks will never wash away. Eventually you will arrive at the base of the eastern hills. Climb to the top, and on the other side, looking towards the Red Sea, there will be a temple and an altar containing a golden serpent. No one but us would have reason to suspect its presence. If the temple were discovered and traced back to us, you know the consequences.'

'Our names would be erased, a proper burial denied, and thus our essence would cease to exist.' Kesi scoffed, as if she felt Qetu should not have bothered bringing up such an obvious fact. 'However, we need not worry, as the power of Apep will keep our temple hidden from prying eyes.'

'That much I assumed.' Qetu looked around the marshes, and the anguished look returned to his face. 'I will need to go back to our leader for clarification on the riddle. It makes little sense to me and is far too vague.'

'Who can say?' Kesi shrugged. 'Legend goes that the past followers had to hide the relic in a rush right after they found it. They then wrote a riddle for posterity so that it could be found and used when the time was right.

'And until then dark magic hides it from the sight of gods.'

'Exactly. And I don't see how our leader will have any special answers.'

Qetu wiped sweat off his brows. 'It's worth a try. I must go to him tonight. Tomorrow morning he's visiting the temple to speak with Apep.'

As if this could be any easier, Sahu thought. All he needed to do was follow Qetu, hear about the riddle, and make it to Apep's temple in time to find out what the Followers had planned. Perhaps he might even learn how they would help Apep overthrow Amun-Ra. By the time he met up with Neferure, they'd have the whole mystery solved.

Sahu followed silently a few yards behind the vizier. Reeds brushed against his fur as he moved through the marsh. Ducks took to the air, and his mouth watered at the sight. Sahu wished he were stalking one of them. Instead he continued his stealthy pursuit as Qetu strode out of the marsh and into the outskirts of the city, towards his hidden master.

Not long had he walked before a realization shot through Sahu's mind: he was already within housecat territory. Although Qetu suspected nothing, he looked as though he was still far from his destination.

I'll follow him just a little further, thought Sahu. *I must know where he's going and who he is meeting. Perhaps no one will recognize me this far from Karnak Temple.*

Too quickly the houses began to consist of two storeys instead of just one, and the streets looked better kept. Sahu felt uneasy. How much further would Qetu travel? How close to Karnak would he come? Was the explanation to the riddle worth risking his life over? Sahu thought not. He considered turning back, yet he could not bring himself to do so. His eyes glanced in all directions, checking to see if he had been spotted by anyone. Some cats were in the streets, but none paid any attention to him. A strong feeling to look upwards spread through his body. What he saw caused his eyes to widen and his heart to quicken.

Three cats looked down upon him from a rooftop. Sahu drew a sharp breath. He had once known the largest of them. The others he had never seen before. One had intense olive-green eyes with which he scrutinized the slightest of Sahu's expressions. A garnet amulet rested upon that cat's neck.

'Over there.' The largest cat pointed with his eyes in Sahu's direction. 'I know him. His name is Sahu, and he was supposed have been buried with the high priest who recently died. He used to be a stray. It seems he is one again.'

Sahu quickened his pace. He hoped to make it past the building and out of sight before the three cats came to any threatening conclusions. One spoke up in a feisty voice. 'The night the fire occurred in the high priest's house, I saw a cat who looked quite like him running for his life. He trailed a scent of smoke and ash.'

'I heard the other cats in the house died trying to wake Akhotep,' the large cat continued. 'It seems Sahu did not have the loyalty or faithfulness to do the same.'

'So he is a betrayer of Ma'at,' a vibrant third voice declared. 'A betrayer of the goddess of order, truth, and justice.'

Sahu considered turning back, then refused to alter his direction. Seeming fearful would only serve to further presume him guilty, and they had already caught sight of him.

'I don't know if I'd go that far...' said the feisty voiced cat.

The eye of Horus flew down from the rooftop as a tongue of liquid fire. Two feline eyes blazed, and a set of paws levelled out upon the street.

'Strays are forbidden from entering this city, and betrayers will meet their end upon the scales in the underworld.'

A betrayer? Who was this small cat who thought he

knew everything and personally owned Thebes? He must be Khakhati—the cat of Per-Maahes Neferure had spoken of. With his aristocratic and critical demeanour, Sahu could understand why the strays greatly disapproved of him. His olive-green eyes still held sparks of amber from his days as a kitten. In build he was slight, looking as if he'd just reached adulthood that day. He could not possibly have the strength to fight while wearing his heavy amulet. It would weigh his body to the ground. Sahu didn't have time for his nonsense.

'I thought kittens were to respect their elders,' he said, readying himself to walk down the next street.

Claws and teeth rushed at his face.

Sahu ducked and slid to the side. For a breath he watched Khakhati sail through the air and land upon his prior ground. With quick footing, Khakhati shifted direction and continued his assault.

Wind blew through the land, and it fed the battle like it would a wildfire.

Khakhati attacked anew, rushing, clawing, and biting. Dust rose like smoke with every step they took. Sharp claws grazed over Sahu's right haunch as he spun around in a semicircle. For a breath their eyes met, veiled behind a cloud of dust. Khakhati's glance ignited. He leapt in the air and came down upon Sahu as a hawk out of the clouds, pinning him to the ground. Sahu rolled onto his back and blocked his body with his paws, then bit at Khakhati's neck. A sharp yowl pierced the air, and Khakhati backed off.

Sahu took that opportunity to slip away into the twilight. He would have to defeat Khakhati another time.

Khakhati did not lack skill, but Sahu had been raised a street fighter and possessed more cunning than most of the strays Khakhati had faced.

His opportunity to hear about the riddle had been lost. Instead he would search out the snake tracks and find his way to the temple of Apep during the night. As he headed back towards the outer city, keeping to the growing shadows of dusk, he could hear Khakhati's resonant voice in the distance.

'A disease of one part of the body can easily set the rest off-balance. No wonder that with their wretched hearts the strays are the first to succumb to this plague. Tell all the housecats to kill *any* stray who tries to enter this city, whether or not they are ill, and to be on the lookout especially for Sahu. We must make an example of him.'

CHAPTER 9

Inner Sanctum

THE SUN HAD vanished. A blanket of storm and cloud veiled the sky. Lightning flashed, backlighting a stone serpent reaching to the sky, devouring a stone sun. The air was bitingly cold, and the land was parched with thirst. Neferure was a wandering spirit, lost upon the earth, unnoticed and without the warmth of a home. She was unable to interact with her environment or leave it. Other lost spirits roamed the land helplessly, for they all knew that the afterworld also stood in ruin. The Reed Fields of Aaru had dried up.

Bones lay strewn on the ground. They were contorted as though the people had died in agony. Neferure had nowhere else to turn. Her spirit floated over stone statues of gods and men, felled and broken. The desert had conquered fertile land. A terrifying roar rumbled deep in the ground, and the earth shivered. She drifted above what had once been the Nile. The life of Egypt had run dry.

Upon the West Bank a skeleton of a cat lay before an open tomb, encircled by a cobra.

A single star in the east broke through the clouds, and Neferure's set her gaze upon it. The star enveloped her in light. Filled with power and might, her spirit rose toward the sky. Her eyes blazed with resolve. The stone serpent shrunk. Fear and awe were now carved into its features.

Neferure woke. Her heart beat as if she'd run to the edge of Thebes without stopping. She stretched out a paw and gripped the soft linen with her claws. No thought needed to be given to the dream's interpretation; it showed how the world would be if Apep defeated Amun-Ra.

She thought back to the moment when the star had broken through the clouds. Did it have any connection to the river of light that had streamed out from beyond the horizon? Doubtful. The star had given her power, whereas the river of light had made her vulnerable. If there was no connection between the two concepts, then what, she wondered, had been the star's significance in her dream?

The storm of her nightmare continued to burden her. She stood up, awaking her muscles with a deep stretch, and briskly groomed her fur.

Out through the wooden columns and doorways she headed until she could see the stars glimmering like bright spirits in the black sky. A few deep breaths of fresh air cleansed her lungs, cleared her mind and chased away all remnant shadows from her heart. She took her time meandering to the garden until she came upon the familiar lotus pool. Neferure looked through the water at the closed lotus buds. They waited patiently for the light of Amun-Ra to return to the land, confident that it would. The surface of the water reflected a cat running towards her. It ran so softly that its paws seemed to skim the earth. Neferure looked up, and she met eye to eye with Ahmes. Something was wrong.

Ahmes spoke up at once, not waiting till she reached her destination. 'Neferure, I have news that you must hear.'

'What is it?' Neferure asked.

As she reached the end of the pool where Neferure was seated, Ahmes slowed her gait and then came to an abrupt stop. She did not sit down, hesitating before voicing her news. 'I was speaking with Khakhati, and he told to me of a strange incident.' Ahmes's voice cracked. 'Khakhati said he fought with "a horrible cat without dignity or self-respect who is a betrayer of Ma'at",' she said, quoting his very words. 'This cat he speaks of did not hold true to his duties towards Karnak Temple.'

Neferure's breathing paused. Something awful had happened to Sahu.

'This cat,' Ahmes continued, 'betrayed Akhotep to keep his own life. Now he is banished from our territory. He will meet death if he returns. Khakhati said it was an extreme judgement called for by an extreme situation. He must send a message to the strays.'

Already Neferure knew what Ahmes would say next.

'That cat is Sahu.'

Neferure's heart fluttered. What Ahmes and Khakhati did not know was that Sahu was banished from stray territory, under similar threats. Her breaths became deep and laboured as her chest tightened with anger. Raw power flowed through her muscles as she thought of lashing out at Khakhati for his idiocy. Her bite wound throbbed for the first time since her attack, and for a moment the muscles in that leg quivered.

Ahmes deciphered the look on Neferure's face. 'You already knew?'

'Yes,' Neferure snapped, 'but you could have broken it to me in a nicer way, or are you now preying on the emotions of other cats instead of mice?'

Surprised by her own words, Neferure reflected on images of Khakhati's fight with the strays. She remembered their bizarre behaviour and quickness to anger. Such an intense feeling of anger was quite unusual for her. The plague had been passed to her.

Neferure had no time for illness and thus forcefully calmed herself. 'Never mind, it is Khakhati who angers me. He judges long before he thinks.'

Ahmes was bothered little by the anger Neferure had shown, for she clearly had other concerns on her mind. 'Why didn't you tell me what you knew?' she demanded. 'Does this have anything to do with that "Book of Apep" Heqaib is translating?'

Neferure's claws unsheathed and dug into the soil. 'He told you?'

With her ears perked, Ahmes scrutinized every minuscule detail in Neferure's expression. 'What are you hiding from me?'

'I can't tell you.' Neferure stared at the ground. 'There is a conspirator among us.'

'What are you talking about? Who is conspiring against what?'

'I can't tell you.'

Intense silence spread through the air. 'Are you accusing me of being this conspirator?' Ahmes said. Her ears flattened against her head, and she shrunk back onto her paws in disbelief. 'I would like to know what I'm conspiring against.'

Neferure found Ahmes' display of emotion and reason convincing. Her friend was never one to put the thought required into lying. Half of Ahmes's mind was always spent alert for the next hunt. However, Neferure reminded herself, there were only two cats in Thebes who wore amulets, neither of whom she would normally suspect of working with the Followers. Much caution was needed, even though her friendship hung in the balance.

'Ahmes, I don't think you're part of anything malicious.'

'Then tell me what you're hiding. If I was part of some scheme, then wouldn't I already know what this is all about?'

Neferure's answering silence brought their friendship to a dismal low. Ahmes sighed and moved to her final statement. 'Heqaib is ill.'

Neferure's tail twitched. 'Ill?'

Turning her head away, Ahmes spoke in a quavering voice. 'It must have been one of the mice I gave him.' She met eye to eye with Neferure, fire in her stare. 'Perhaps his sickness was also part of my grand scheme.'

Ahmes gave Neferure moments to voice an explanation or an apology. Upon receiving none, she walked off stiffly through the garden. Neferure was left looking into the night, torn between anger at Khakhati, hurt from the fight with Ahmes, sadness about Heqaib's illness and fear for Sahu's life.

By the time Neferure found herself inside Karnak it was deep into the night. She stood at the crossroads of the temple's two axes, outside the wall of the fourth pylon.

Behind her loomed the much larger third pylon and the grand hypostyle hall. In front of her, past the gateway of the fourth pylon, was the room no cat had ever entered—the inner sanctum of Amun-Ra.

A few steps away stood the heart of Thebes, home of the most revered god in all of Egypt. Neferure had heard that the pharaohs had gone always directly to the mouth of Amun-Ra for guidance and instructions. As far as she was concerned, nothing stopped her from doing the same. Although the sun god was shunning Ramesses, perhaps he would speak with her. She knew the thick wooden doors of the inner sanctum would be closed and sealed until the priests opened them in the morning. She would wait in the shadows of the temple until dawn came.

With silent steps Neferure passed beyond the fourth pylon and entered into the shadow of a mystery. Her pupils easily compensated for the lack of light. Whereas any human would have been lost in the dark, Neferure's eyes enabled her to distinguish colourless shapes and forms.

To her right and left stood the bases of Queen Hatshepsut's obelisks. They had both been walled up, her name hidden, under the order of Thutmose III, the early part of whose reign Hatshepsut had taken for her own. Behind the walled obelisks two short rows of columns stretched to the north and to the south.

Neferure looked forward at yet another pylon, the fifth, just ahead. Assuming no danger, she walked the short distance towards her new destination. As she passed that gateway she found herself inside a narrow vestibule, its thick stone walls looming eerily on either side. She carefully tested the air currents with her whiskers and put her nose to the incense-laden air. Nothing warned her of any threats and so she ventured further.

Upon exiting the vestibule, Neferure entered into an antechamber. Before her stood the final pylon along the east-west axis, the smallest of all the gateways. Two cedar doors inlayed with gold and electrum stood before her. Inscribed upon them, in the same metals, were hieroglyphs she wished she could have read. Few humans ever saw beyond those doors.

A closer look through the dim lighting revealed that the left door was ever so slightly ajar. Neferure hooked her claws into the thick wood and pulled at it, using every last muscle in her small body. Inch by inch the heavy door slowly creaked open and she managed to create an opening large enough to squeeze through.

The steady warmth of torchlights washed across Neferure's fur as she stepped beyond the last pylon. The fires created enough light to distinguish the images and hieroglyphs on the walls. Although she could not read the words, Neferure recognized several depictions of Thutmose III. Yet another pair of column-filled chambers stood on either side of her. Compared to the grand hypostyle hall they appeared small and quaint. On either side of the doorway into the northern chamber stood a six metre tall statue carved of red granite. One was of Amun and the other was of Amunet—a female version of the great god. Torchlight flickered upon their faces. No matter how the fire's light played upon their features, the faces of the gods never appeared angry or vengeful. Such was the mastery of Egyptian artisans.

Directly ahead lay the inner sanctum. Neferure noted the wax seal was broken, and the ropes that bound the two metal bolts together were cut. One door had been opened wide enough for a cat to pass through. Although the opportunity was to Neferure's advantage, it did not stop her from worrying how, and why, it had happened. It certainly could not have been done through carelessness.

Two rectangular granite columns loomed like guardians standing before the inner sanctum. One bore three papyrus heads. Three lotus heads were carved into the other. They were symbols of Lower and Upper Egypt. Neferure cautiously advanced beyond them, then passed through the heavy doors. She drew breath as she set her paws upon the most sacred ground in Thebes.

A single flickering ray of torchlight emanating from beyond the doors split apart the darkness. Golden stars were painted upon a blue ceiling lower than any other in the temple, giving the impression that the cosmos shone just within reach. Neferure followed the ray of torchlight. It led her past the area intended for offerings before bringing her face to face with Amun-Ra.

Upon the altar sat the god's small, intricately carved statue and his majestic golden solar barque. The statue itself had been created to house the soul of the sun god so that he could inhabit the land.

Amun's small statue of gold gleamed in the dull lighting as a sun engulfed in the veil of night. Neferure didn't know how to explain it, but somehow there was a power to that statue, a presence spreading far beyond the shrouded darkness and stone walls. Warmth flickered through the air like a thousand flames, both passive and powerful. Incense had soaked into the very walls, and the stones echoed with hymns repeated through the centuries. This was the peak of the Mound of Creation, keeping away the primeval chaos of the desert from reclaiming the fertile soils of Egypt. The room itself seemed to give a thousand answers hidden in a thousand questions; surely hers was among them.

'Amun, please offer me guidance,' Neferure spoke in a hushed voice. 'Everything around me is falling apart. Sahu faces either exile or death. Apep's servants come closer and closer to bringing evil to power. Disease spreads through Thebes and my own body. We have no hope but for Heqaib and his translations. He is ill, and I fear he will not be able to tell me enough information in time. Tell me, what am I to do? Why do I see the river of light at sunrise?'

The crackling of the flames in the hallway seemed only to deepen the silence within the inner sanctum. Neferure waited patiently, but no words were uttered directly from the mouth of Amun-Ra. She was a cat of no lineage, unworthy to speak with the great god Amun-Ra. Yet with the fate of Egypt at stake, she'd expected an answer. His rejection darkened her mood to despair.

'Surely you can answer my questions. Why do you remain silent? This battle is against you of all gods.'

Anger flared within her stronger than all the torches of the temple.

'How much must I beg for an answer? I will do what-ever is needed if only I could know what it is. How can I accomplish a task that is kept hidden from me? What was

Akhotep's secret?' Neferure listened to the voice of nothingness. 'Tell me!'

Her words were swallowed up in Amun-Ra's silence.

Heavy-lidded eyes drew her face to the ground. A slew
of fears, doubts, and uncertainties drained all hope from
her body. Neferure felt as a last leaf waiting to fall from a
dying tree, powerless to stop a fate she knew was upon her.
The plague would spread alongside Apep's rising. Perhaps
the fault was not with Ramesses. Perhaps the view of the
gods was clouded.

With paws as heavy as the stone around her, Neferure
gave up on divine assistance and walked out past the heavy
wooden doors, exiting the inner sanctum of Amun-Ra.

Neferure's blood pulsed sluggishly in her veins. Her
muscles were wrought iron, and her lungs moved heavy
as a bowstring. She thought of Sahu being chased into
the desert. His future looked as lifeless as the sands upon
which he now ran.

Maybe, Neferure thought, the path of the sun through
the sky mirrored the path of Egypt. Perhaps a period of
darkness was coming upon them, and there was nothing
they could do to stop it, no more than they could stop
Amun-Ra from sailing through the underworld each night.

Absorbed entirely in her own thoughts, Neferure
scarcely noticed she had walked all the way back to the
fourth pylon.

A deep, baritone voice stopped her in her tracks.

'What do you mean, the seal has been broken?' the voice
questioned. 'Were you not there when it happened? Were
you not guarding those doors?'

Side-stepping into the shadows and peering through the gateway, Neferure came to realize that Khesef-hra, the high priest of Amun-Ra, was speaking with another of the temple's priests. The second man seemed more than eager to defend his actions.

'I was on guard,' he quickly explained. 'Some trickery is at work here. I had not fallen asleep, but I heard a strange voice calling me from behind. The voice sounded like many whispers, both friendly and ominous. I turned to find its source, but my eyes beheld nothing but shadow. When I looked back, the seal on the door was broken and the ropes cut.'

Khesef-hra stared at the other priest, letting his silence separate fact from fiction. 'And no one had entered the inner sanctum while you fetched me?'

'Of that I am not sure,' the other priest replied. 'I feel certain, though, that nothing was taken.'

Without another word, Khesef-hra turned and walked towards the inner sanctum. The other priest spun on his heels and followed closely behind. The pair strode through the pylons without noticing Neferure. Within seconds, they were out of her sight. Only the sounds of their footsteps carried back through the halls and chambers.

One thing was left for Neferure to do. She needed to make sure her intended meeting place with Sahu, later that day, was still safe. Her body tightened as she realized she had no way to warn him if it wasn't.

For the second time in two days, Neferure travelled to the edge of Thebes. As she walked along the dusty and dark streets, she soon became aware of an unnerving pattern. A single cat was seated upon every two or three of the low rooftops bordering the city, watching the distance and scanning the edges of stray territory. Neferure thought back to what Ahmes said about Khakhati. He seemed to have taken quite a dislike towards the strays since he arrived. Now it appeared he had set up outposts with sentinels all along the Theban border.

She quickened her pace till she reached her destination. To her horror, Neferure discovered that the marsh, the abandoned mud brick house, and the cavern opening all lay in plain view of Khakhati's main outpost. Sahu would be spotted long before he arrived at their meeting place.

The two-story building used for the main outpost was unusually tall for that area of the city. It gave a greater view of the surrounding area than the lower houses did. Several cats were stationed at that one outpost.

Khakhati himself was looking far into the distance. His strong voice carried easily through the night air. 'I have heard rumours that the betrayer frequents these areas. Likely he will soon appear again. He will not dare enter so far into the city as he did the day I fought him, and if he tries he will die before he has a chance to regret it.'

Neferure stood unnoticed. Her anger towards Khakhati flared, ignited by the first blood-red rays of the rising sun, intensifying alongside the morning light. Red beams of light boiled to orange before Neferure recalled what else came along with the sunrise.

She thought to run inside one of the old houses to avoid another unpleasant mystical experience. With a flash of anger she decided against it. Neferure no longer cared to avoid the river of light. Too much had gone wrong for her, and all without any outside help, divine or otherwise. Only she would be able to help herself and Sahu. Only she had control over her own destiny and her own experiences in life.

In defiance of her vulnerability, Neferure walked towards one of the cross streets, where the walls of houses did not block her view of the horizon. She looked at the point where the sun met with the earth, trying with all internal strength to resist what she feared.

More powerfully than ever before, Neferure felt and saw the river of light rushing towards her and the land.

CHAPTER 10

Before the Star Rises

SAHU STOOD AT the apex of a high Theban hill, facing the morning sun, looking down upon Apep's temple. A rather tiring journey through the desert, and foraging for water at the intermittent wells, was now behind him. If he had expected to see a great monument of beauty for his efforts, he would have been gravely disappointed. Sahu saw exactly what he imagined—a hideous structure, so ugly that it dulled the surrounding beauty of nature and bled all colour from the world around it.

The temple was built of grey granite and sandstone, worn down by time and desert storms. Clearly it had existed for many centuries but had lain forgotten and abandoned; sand still partially concealed it. It stood without the colour or intricately defined hieroglyphs and images of Karnak. If there had ever been writings upon the stone, they were long gone. Winds tried relentlessly to wash away the temple's existence.

The architecture and layout of the temple was as twisted as a coiled serpent about to strike. An avenue guarded by rearing stone snakes wound down the hill and led to a crumbled pylon that opened into a disorganized hypostyle hall. Mixed and matched columns held up a roof in a state of collapse. The columns looked as though they had been stolen from greater temples and appallingly defaced. What light came through the broken roof hit the floor in grotesque patterns. Beyond that mockery of Karnak, a short path led directly to the inner sanctum of Apep.

Sahu noticed the inner temple had suffered the most from time. Only a few short, broken walls surrounded an altar of hematite. Around the altar coiled a serpent of gold. Its garnet eyes seemed to flame under the morning light, as if in anger at the rebirth of Amun-Ra. Oddly enough, it appeared to Sahu that the serpent and his altar were as new as the day itself. If it was not new, Sahu could not comprehend what forces had prevented the statue from being stolen. Man's greed for gold was legendary.

Sahu stole a quick glance over his shoulders, looking towards the southwest. A small black speck caught his eye. He watched the minuscule figure until he was certain it was following the serpent tracks. One of the Followers was heading towards his destination. By Qetu's account, this was the leader of Apep's followers.

With flawless balance Sahu descended the barren sandy hill. He leapt fluidly from one rocky outcropping onto another, scaling his way down towards the temple, searching until he found a suitable hiding spot. Without assessing its safety, he crawled inside a small crevice in the hill. From there he could look towards the temple yet remain hidden from all but the sharpest vision. Anxious, Sahu waited in the darkness, watching Ra's solar barque sail through the sky.

Time drifted as slowly as a morning fog floating across the Nile. Sahu wondered many things about the distant past. He questioned how the followers of Apep had first come to honour such an evil, and if the same lies were used to ensnare them each time. Did Apep wait until generations had passed and all who lived had forgotten about the ill fates that had likely plagued his previous followers?

Sounds of heavy footsteps treading upon rock and sand coursed through the air. A shadow glided over the ground. Sahu looked up and saw a tall human passing in front of his sight, wearing a brown cloak. The stranger's face was hidden behind a cowl. His hands, the only things visible, looked powerful and comfortable with a sword. His gait was regal, assured, and slightly familiar.

Sahu willed the stranger, undoubtedly a man, to turn towards him. Taking confident steps, the stranger scanned his environment and, once he was certain he was alone, dropped his cowl. Sahu's heart sank and his ears drew flat. He recognized the man instantly.

It was Khesef-hra.

The priest had always been kind to the servants, and Akhotep had treated the man like a son as well as a successor. All of Thebes had trusted him fully to carry on in Akhotep's footsteps, to keep the presence of Amun-Ra strong within the land. This was treason of the highest order—treason against the gods themselves. The highest priest of Karnak was also the secret leader of Apep's cult. Now it was clear why sickness and disease plagued the lands. Sahu was surely looking at the very man responsible for Akhotep's death.

The high priest had changed much since Sahu last saw

him. His face was ravaged by age. Each line was etched
with determination, every feature chiselled with pride, but
his chafed feet ploughed through the burning sands as
though they were bound in iron shackles. Pride and greed
had conquered his once meek soul and turned his living
heart to stone.

Khesef-hra did not bother walking through the temple
by the standard entrance. He entered the ruined inner sanctum by stepping through a break in the dilapidated walls.
He stopped shortly before the altar and removed a silver
ankh from a cord around his neck. Set into the centre was a
small round piece of meteorite, the stones that fell from the
heavens. The high priest of Amun-Ra placed the ankh in a
slot upon the altar. He aligned the black stone to the north,
where the star Thuban, the star of Apep, would appear in
the night sky. The instant he let go of his tool a hollow and
terrifying roar shook the sands.

Sahu's ears flattened, his eyes widened, and he shrunk
back until he was pressed against the stone at the back of
his hideaway. With all his will he summoned Bast to be by
his side.

The deep, baritone voice of Khesef-hra bounced off the
rocks as though the earth refused to hear him speak. 'My
Lord,' he said. 'Everything is in place. We need only final-
ize the plans.'

Apep's hoarse voice answered, vibrating through the
ground. 'What of The Word?'

'We are extremely close to finding the amulet, my Lord.
We will have it for you by tonight.'

Finding The Word? Sahu wondered, forgetting his fear.

How could a single word be of use to Apep, and what did it have to do with an amulet? He peered out from between the stones, as if finding a better view could help further his understanding.

Sahu's thoughts were broken by another loud roar, splintering the silence into a thousand shards.

'You have every right to be angry for my insolence,' Khesef-hra's voice quavered, 'but I have destroyed Akhotep, and his secret is hidden. No one can ever use it now to oppose you. We have nothing but time.'

'Time is something I'll always have,' the deathly voice boomed. 'You, on the other hand, do not. You know that it is far more difficult and dangerous for me to rise on this earth when the star of Isis shines down upon me. If you do not bring me The Word before Sopdet rises in the sky, then you will join Akhotep in Amenti.'

The air thickened under the presence of the god of chaos, pressing down upon Sahu's breaths as an iron weight. His thoughts moved like a dying wind, straining to reach old areas of his memory. Barely he recalled that the star Sopdet was due to rise the next morning, after seventy days of absence. Sahu struggled to understand how manifesting on the earth would help Apep defeat Amun-Ra.

The many lines on Khesef-hra's face wrote the purest expression of fear. 'I cannot join Akhotep in Amenti. After swearing my oath to you, I would never survive the trial under Osiris. To him you are the greatest of all evils.'

'That's why you must find me The Word. Under my rule you shall have everlasting life and power.'

'I need more time.'

'You need only what I give you. If you desire more, then you are as worthless as those who are not my followers.'

'My apologies, my Lord. Please forgive me.' Khesef-hra bowed low to the ground until his bald head touched the hot sands. In that pose he remained for many breaths. Then his eyebrows shot up, and his head lifted to meet them. 'Through my own means,' Khesef-hra continued, 'I have had a wax figure of yours placed in the inner sanctum of Karnak. When the time comes, one of your manifestations will rise upon the earthly throne of Ra.'

The silence that followed suggested Apep was unimpressed. Khesef-hra seemed pleased enough that he had kept his god from further anger. Stiffly, he rose back onto his tired feet and spoke once more. 'The other priests believe I have already performed the ritual Banishing of Apep. They all believe Egypt is safely protected. No one can stop you now that Akhotep's secret is lost.'

'I will not take that chance. You underestimate species other than your own...'

'Perhaps in the meantime,' Khesef-hra continued, 'I can tell the other Followers to deliver incense and food to your altar.'

'I need no earthly goods,' Apep replied. 'I thrive solely on my own power. The sound of my roar fills my heart with strength equal to no other god. Only their combined effort keeps me at bay.'

'I know of your pain,' Khesef-hra said. 'Soon I will not have to serve your enemy.'

In a voice thick with suppressed anger, Apep gave his final orders. 'Go now, and do not return again unless you have found The Word. I tire of being suppressed by Amun-Ra and his servants who call themselves gods.'

Khesef-hra bowed before the altar and then turned away.

Sahu scarcely waited for the high priest to walk out of sight before he bolted out of his hideaway and ran straight towards Thebes, keeping to depressions in the landscape so that he would not be seen. The enormity of the danger everyone was in dawned upon him. He had to tell Neferure who the leader was. She was the only one who would believe him. He would have to brave Khakhati's wrath, though it might be simple enough to avoid him. Khakhati, after all, could not know and see all.

CHAPTER 11

Taking Guard

'THIS WAR OF yours against the strays is not the answer,' Neferure said to Khakhati as she stood on top of the roof that served as his main outpost. 'A great evil is behind this plague, not strays.'

Khakhati retained his calm and collected demeanour, keeping his eyes trained on the horizon. His tail was curled loosely at his side, but his ears rotated ceaselessly. He made no gestures in response to Neferure's verbal lashing. 'I have come to realize strays are the evil,' he said. 'What would make you believe otherwise?'

Neferure thought about the true evils—the Followers, their secret meeting, Apep. There was so much to say, but no definite answers to give. She recalled her memory of the cat carrying the serpent figurine. Who was that cat? Who among her own species could she not trust?

'Nothing,' she replied. 'It's nothing but a feeling.'

Without breaking his guard, Khakhati laughed at Neferure's foolishness. 'I'm sorry, but feelings alone do not make strays innocent.' His right ear swivelled backwards in the direction of the stairway. Neferure turned and saw Ahmes set foot upon the rooftop.

'Now, for your own protection,' Khakhati continued, 'let the proper lineages do their job.'

Neferure swiftly became aware of one crucial concept. If Khakhati spoke with Ahmes, her affiliation with Sahu might be given away. She took her chances and stayed upon the rooftop, hoping Ahmes would not betray her. A new plot formed quickly in her head.

'Let me do my part then,' Neferure said, breaking into Khakhati's conversation. 'Let me do my part so I can free up time for you. I wish to be of some aid and to be considered helpful rather than a nuisance.'

Khakhati's whiskers pressed against his face, and his ears flattened out to the side. 'What do you suppose you can do?'

'I can take up your position of guard,' she said. 'Watching for strays is something simple that any cat could do. Obviously your talent is needed for greater things, and I realize now I was wrong to doubt your judgement.'

For a long while, Khakhati eyed her suspiciously. Neferure held her ground, ignoring the disgusted look upon Ahmes's face, holding out until Khakhati gave her the slightest of nods.

Stepping aside, Khakhati let Neferure take his place. She sat down immediately and began scanning the distance, only she was not looking for sick strays. She was judging from what angles and directions Sahu would approach, if he dared to come back at all.

Minutes passed by with Khakhati skeptically watching how Neferure handled the job. When at last he seemed satisfied, he gave a speech.

'If we deviate from the ideals of the goddess Ma'at, if we turn away from order, truth, and justice, then those very things will leave this land. The chaos of the desert will overtake the fertile valley. We cannot let the strays into our lands, for the disorder of their ways will turn our city into a barren waste. At all costs do not let down your guard.'

He descended the stairway and exited through the house. Ahmes followed. Neither paid Neferure any further attention.

Hours passed as Neferure maintained her guard. Still and silent she sat upon the rooftop, observing every shadow around her and watching any movement with unceasing vigilance.

A cerulean blue sky shimmered above the radiant green foliage of the Nile Valley. The scorching sun beat down upon her back and warmed the mud brick roof enough even to be sensed through the tough pads on her paws. With her sharp eyes, Neferure traced the strict lines separating irrigated farmland from that of the pale green savannah lying beyond.

A harper's song sailed across the sky. His skilful hands played an elegant melody to which his wife sang as she weeded their small garden. She gave voice to the love between Isis and Osiris.

Nothing of importance appeared to be happening. Evening was far away and Neferure did not expect to see Sahu until then. Boredom fatigued her mind, bringing her to wonder if her guard had begun far too early.

Visible to her right and left were a few cats stationed at other posts. Looking at them all, lined up in a row, made Khakhati's guard seem ludicrous and wasteful. She figured he overestimated the threat of the strays and that his guard was more for a display of power than for protection.

Curling her front paw and bringing it to her mouth, Neferure began washing her face and ears. The cat stationed to her far left shot her a warning glance. With her throat parched with thirst and her fur demanding attention, she disregarded him.

Anger lapped like a tongue of flame. Fear dowsed her rage once she recalled the symptoms of the plague. Neferure worked to convince herself she was not ill.

A sharp, shrill squeal bounced off her ears. Looking down, her eyes beheld a snake darting towards a mouse, nearly securing itself a meal.

Each of Khakhati's sentinels searched out the source of the noise.

Because of their divided attention, they did not see what Neferure saw as she glanced back at the expanse of the desert and savannah. Their eyes were oblivious to the dark speck running across the sands, pausing upon sight of the guard and then taking a far less direct route towards the city. Neferure breathed thanks to Bast for the timing.

Sahu had adeptness for survival beyond that of most cats. Neferure knew he would not halt his path towards the city. She felt certain that Sahu was there, defying the unrelenting eyes of Khakhati's sentinels, slinking behind rocks and hugging low to slants in the terrain. She was not in the least surprised that she soon saw a flash of silver within the small cavern itself, easily mistaken for a glint of light off the Nile.

Thoughts raced through her mind as she tried to decide how best to reach Sahu and prevent the other cats from detecting him.

Glare from the sun reflected off an amulet. Gasping, Neferure turned to her right and scrutinized the amulet's moving shape. She could tell it was attached to a collar that was, in turn, attached to a cat. Was it Ahmes? She truly hoped it was. If Ahmes saw Sahu it posed far less danger, for she might not heed Khakhati's wishes of vengeance.

Neferure did not take her eyes off the stone until it came within clear sight. It was carved as the eye of Horus. Her heart sank. Khakhati was heading in Sahu's direction.

Soon he would be close to the marsh and the cavern. She could not speak to Sahu or reach him in time to warn him without Khakhati's sentinels noticing her absence.

The harper's song quickened. His wife now sang about the murder of Osiris. A vulture took flight and circled in the sky, eyeing those below.

Khakhati walked down the streets, tail held high in the air, turning his head from side to side, surveying the houses as though they were all extensions of his own personal territory.

Without hesitation, he turned sharply and made his way towards a wooden door.

'I am Khakhati of Per-Maahes,' he meowed, 'and I demand entrance to this house.' He was checking in with the cat on the roof above—the same cat, stationed at her left, who had disapproved of Neferure's grooming.

Neferure glanced back and forth between the cavern and the wooden door. Khakhati's patience was wearing thin. No one had opened the door for him, and he had resorted to scratching at the wood with his sharp claws, making a horrible screeching noise in the process.

'Let me in!' Khakhati demanded.

Sharply the door swung open.

'Stop meowing! Can't you just decide whether you want to stay in or out?' came a woman's voice from the darkness. 'Oh,' she said, seconds later, 'you're of Per-Maahes? Come in.'

'That's what I've been saying,' Khakhati replied indignantly as he strutted into her house. Within moments he was upon the rooftop drilling his sentinel for information.

Neferure watched from the corner of her eyes. She only caught the last phrase clearly. 'Check the cavern again,' Khakhati said. 'Perhaps the betrayer himself or another stray has returned without our knowing. I will cover your guard.'

Neferure focused her gaze upon a random but distant rocky outcropping. 'Strays!' she yowled. 'Behind the rocks! Strays are making their way towards the city!'

'We must stop them!' cried the cat to her right as he followed Neferure's line of sight.

In one synchronized movement, the line of sentinels plunged down from their posts in a waterfall of fur. Khakhati himself led the way into the distance.

Claws scraping, Neferure launched herself off the roof. She flew two stories, muscles in her front legs absorbing all the impact as she hit the earth. She waited moments for the other cats to overtake her before running directly towards the cavern.

Mud splattered upon her golden fur and tall reeds whacked her in the face as she entered the marsh. She glanced frequently over her shoulder for Khakhati.

As she came upon the cavern, her legs gave way, and she fell face first into the shallow, murky water.

Sahu jumped into the marsh and ran towards her. 'Neferure?! What's wrong?'

She picked herself out of the mud and shook her fur, ignoring his question. 'Sahu! Come with me. It isn't safe to wait here. Follow me closely and silently.'

Without a sound or further questioning, Sahu followed. He kept pressed to the earth, peeking out into the open before moving forward from the cavern.

'Hurry!' Neferure urged as she looked back at the guard. The other cats had nearly reached the rocky outcropping.

Speeding up, Sahu and Neferure took off into the city. Their muddy paws left behind a telltale path, fading as the sun bleached the road. They took many turns through the streets, skidding past corners and backtracking often to confuse anyone who tried to track them down by scent. Usually they kept to the river, running along the lands bordering the Nile.

As they edged on through the sun-drenched streets, Sahu glanced about more frequently. 'In case you haven't noticed, we're running into the inner city—a place where I'm not exactly welcome anymore.'

'We can't run towards Khakhati and his sentinels.'

Sahu looked above the walls of houses and towards the

giant pylons and obelisks of Karnak. For a brief moment, he looked to the ground. 'Khakhati knows who I am, and what I've done. He also knows I'm a stray.'

With her lips pulled back, Neferure glanced at Sahu. 'I've heard about that incident.'

Every stride drew them nearer to Karnak, the mega-lithic obelisks beckoning them forward until all the houses disappeared from view and they ran alongside the outer wall of the temple.

'Khakhati may have found out about our connection,' Sahu said. 'That places you in danger too, whether or not you're seen with me now.'

Neferure stopped in her tracks, again ignoring Sahu's concerns.

The avenue of ram-headed sphinxes loomed before their path, leading from the docking quay into Karnak and separating her and Sahu from the south side of the city. To their left stood the strong walls of Karnak; to their right ran the mighty Nile.

Near the river a large boned cat was scouting for his next meal. Sahu was fast to recognize him. 'That cat knows who I am. We must leave.'

'Quick! We can hide in the vastness of the temple for a while. No one would expect you to return to Karnak.' Without waiting for a reply, she took off towards the grand pylons.

The branches of low growing shrubs combed through their fur as Neferure and Sahu squeezed past the noble-faced stone sphinxes and onto the pathway.

'Neferure, maybe this is not the wisest—'

'We have no time,' she shot back. 'Would you rather swim across the Nile?'

'Preferably not.' Sahu looked down the avenue and towards a small boat coming to dock.

A heavyset man stood up from his seat upon the singular chair on the deck. His linen kilt was stiffly pleated into a triangular shape in front, signifying his job did not require him to do any physical labour. Lumbering to his feet, the man then pointed at one of the many wooden chests before him.

'This is the finest incense in all of Egypt,' he said as his two workers secured the boat to the dock and set in place a plank leading from the deck to the ground. 'Amun will be greatly pleased, provided this time you don't drop any of it.'

One of the workers rolled his eyes, and the other gave a tight-lipped smile. With unsteady hands, they picked up both ends of two poles attached to the chest and lifted it off the boat. They carried the heavy chest down the plank with slow, drudging steps. The chest was decorated by a noble sphinx sitting atop it.

'We can make Khakhati and his guard *think* we swam across the Nile,' Sahu said. 'Because of the plague, few boats are allowing cats onto them; likely this one will be no different. However, if we can run to the edge of the dock, then jump onto the chest of supplies—'

'No scent will be left to trace our steps.' Neferure said, her eyes alight.

Finally confident in a decision of theirs, Sahu set off towards the temple quay and the dock, leading the way down the avenue. Many stone eyes of Amun's sphinxes looked down upon them. The low shrubs concealed their path from the eyes of other cats.

The man leading the way did not give the slightest care when he felt the extra weight of two small cats jump onto the chest of incense. All that came from the mouth of the second man was a slight groan in protest at the extra work-load and a scowl at the two cats. And so Neferure and Sahu were carted off towards the temple of Karnak in a manner befitting royalty, though both were now in exile.

The pair kept as still as possible, hoping any cat in the distance would think they were part of the elaborate carv-ing. The workers seemed as though they were also trying to emulate statues, moving as slowly as if their muscles were made of stone.

'Just eight more months of this,' the man in front droned. 'Just eight more months until I can buy my own fields.'

Vexation grew on Sahu's face and anger on Neferure's.

'I keep telling you,' the second man said, 'if we put all our timber and onions together, we could buy property right now.'

'How many times do we have to go through this?' the first man replied. 'You want to grow emmer wheat and I want to grow barley. Emmer wheat reminds me far too much of my aunt.' He shivered. 'I want nothing to do with it.'

Neferure was despairing about their progress when the heavyset man from the dock reappeared. 'Hurry it up if you want to get paid!'

With swift steps, Neferure and Sahu were carried past the thick walls of the mountainous first pylon and then into the courtyard. They stopped before the second pylon, the doorway into the hypostyle hall. The two men laid the chest down upon the ground and sighed with relief.

In unison, two priests emerged from the shadows of the hypostyle hall, nodding their heads slightly towards the workers. They came forward to take the goods further into the temple. They grasped the poles and lifted the chest.

The priests passed into the secrecy of the hall, taking little notice of Neferure and Sahu. Soundlessly they walked, seemingly floating with their white linen robes nearly touching the ground. Dim light reflected dully upon their shaved heads.

Neferure and Sahu jumped onto the stone floor and skidded off into the depths of the hypostyle hall. Stone columns, thicker and taller than any tree in Egypt, loomed above them. Eventually they reached the far wall, and there they stopped.

Sahu tilted his head. 'He's still here?'

'Who?' Neferure asked as she swivelled around. 'Oh, the old cat. I doubt it matters he's here. We should be safe to talk, at least for a while.'

'We might be among the privileged few to see him cough up a hairball.' Sahu said before beginning his story.

Neferure waited to hear of his recollections. Neither knew a pair of eyes and ears were watching them from the shadows. Not one of them saw the beam of filtered light pass through a garnet stone—an amulet shaped as the eye of Horus, resting upon the chest of a young cat.

CHAPTER 12

The Plan

AS THEY SPOKE, Neferure carefully groomed her displaced and mud-splattered fur. Sahu did not bother doing the same. He was slipping back too comfortably into the appearance of a stray. She moved to nuzzle him, but stopped. Now an outcast as well, was this the image of her own future, should she survive the plague? How long could she hold onto the dignity of a highborn housecat? She wasn't sure she could live a stray's life. She'd found her answers, she'd found Sahu, and she'd just saved him from the housecats. Only now did Neferure realize she had sacrificed everything else in her world.

'What have you found out?' Sahu asked.

'I have found nothing.' Neferure scrunched her face and spat out a mouthful of dry mud. 'I've delivered the scroll to Heqaib, but he's now sick, delaying the deciphering process. However, there is another mystery I need explained.' She closed her eyes for a moment and drew a deep breath, forcing out words bound to unmask her fear. 'Before every sunrise I see a river of light, flowing from beyond the horizon, heading towards me and the land. I—,' she paused. 'I become paralyzed until the light is outshone by the sun.'

Sahu only looked at her. Neferure, impatient for the silence to end, tilted her head to the side, bidding him to speak. He seemed both concerned and taken aback that she had not told him earlier of her troubles.

'How long has this been happening? Why didn't you tell me?' Sahu moved to nuzzle Neferure.

'It only intensified after we met.' A wave of regret washed over Neferure. She shifted weight away from the leg with her bite wound. Surely this was solely her burden to bear. 'We have more pressing matters at hand. What have you learnt?'

Sahu withdrew. 'Khesef-hra is the leader of the Followers.' He shut his eyes for a moment. 'Khesef-hra is the one who killed Akhotep to hide his secret.'

'The new high priest?' The words sounded foreign to Neferure's ears. This betrayal cut deep, yet they had no time to dwell on it. 'What else did you learn?'

'Khesef-hra waits only for The Word.'

'Yes, and why has Apep not given it?'

Sahu shook some dried mud off of his fur. 'Because the one who waits for The Word *is* Apep. He can't give something he hasn't found.'

'How—' Neferure stopped mid-thought. A torch lit inside her mind, as if illuminating a wall of hieroglyphic clues she could finally translate. She searched her memory, recovering the last myth Heqaib had told her—the myth about how Isis learnt Ra's secret name.

'Isis,' said Neferure. 'Isis once learnt the secret name of Amun-Ra, the one that could be used against him.' She shared her knowledge of the story with Sahu. In that instant they both understood the aim of the Followers: to use Ra's secret name to bind his power.

'The Word has something to do with an amulet,' Sahu said. 'I believe Qetu was searching for it in the Nile. He didn't find it, and Apep is angry.'

Neferure's eyes widened; her posture stiffened in anticipation and curiosity. Finally they were reaching some tangible answers. Perhaps there would be a way through *this* after all. 'You mean to say that this powerful secret lies hidden in an amulet?'

'It would seem so,' Sahu said. 'Apep's followers can't deliver the amulet to him in the underworld. He needs to crawl upon the surface of Egypt to touch it, and he will not let any of The Followers learn The Word to tell him. From that word alone they could become as powerful as he.'

Neferure perked her ears, recalling another myth she had once heard from Heqaib. The myth brought more pieces of the mystery together. Her eyes glazed over as she retrieved the tale from her mind.

'When Osiris was killed by his brother Set,' Neferure began, 'Isis wept tears of blood. She fashioned those tears into a Tyet amulet and placed it upon her dead husband's neck. It could be possible that her amulet holds all the knowledge she does, including the secret name of Ra. We must stop The Followers from finding it, and they are surely ahead of us.

Sahu's eyes lit up in revelation. 'We must find Akhotep's secret!'

Neferure looked sharply at him. 'Qetu confirmed it himself: Akhotep's secret is buried with him. We cannot wake the dead.'

'Exactly, and that's why it will be so easy to find.'

'You're trying to say that his secret was something physical?'

'Yes. The ankh he always wore,' Sahu said with certainty. 'It must be opposite to the one Khesef-hra wears, the one he used to contact Apep. That's why The Followers rushed Akhotep's mummification. What better place to hide a secret weapon than inside a tomb?'

Sahu's revelation made sense. Akhotep had always worn his silver ankh around his neck and guarded it with much caution and vigilance. He never took his eyes off of it. Perhaps it was the key to the knowledge they now sought.

'The only way to secure the ankh would be to break into Akhotep's tomb,' Neferure said. 'That lies far out near the Valley of the Kings across the Nile, a valley guarded by the cobra goddess Meretseger, whose assailants always wait upon the earth. You call that easy?' How many lives did Sahu think he had? 'I said easy to find, not easy to *acquire*.'

Neferure looked away, taking moments to come to terms with the path that lay before them. 'I've heard that past the edge of this city there's a man who owns a boat that he uses to ferry people and supplies across the Nile. I hear he is quite eccentric, yet he sails on time every day: to the West Bank every evening and to Thebes just before dawn. The man is still letting cats on board, despite the plague. However, his boat docks in the middle of stray territory.'

'Yes,' said Sahu, 'we will need their support.'

'*Their support?*' Sahu must surely have lost his mind.

'Not long ago you told me the strays refused to accept you back into their ranks. A miracle would be needed to gain their trust.'

A new voice shot out from the shadows. 'I will deal with the strays.'

Dim light from the clerestory windows washed over Khakhati's amulet as he stepped forward from behind a column. Neferure and Sahu exchanged a fearful glance.

Khakhati bowed his head for the slightest moment, signifying he meant no immediate harm. His tail remained high in the air, and his posture was kept both rigid and regal. 'Why didn't you tell me what you knew?'

Neferure arched her spine. 'I didn't consider you trust-worthy.'

Sahu flattened his ears and pressed his whiskers against his face. 'And because last time we met you tried to send me to Amenti.'

'*Tried?*' Khakhati hissed, his teeth gleaming as dull pearls. 'You make it sound as though I wouldn't have suc-ceeded, had you stayed and fought honourably.'

'I fight only battles that need to be fought.' Sahu hissed in return. 'Petty squabbles over strength are not what the gods of Amenti judge us by.'

Venomous eyes met Sahu's. 'I am Khakhati of Per-Maahes. I am a cat of lineage, and the gods favour me. No battle is needed to prove that. If ever you make it to Amenti, you will see it for fact.'

Neferure's heart sank at what she feared was true: that Sahu might never pass the tests of the afterworld. 'How do you plan to help us past the strays?'

'I will give you a weapon,' a fourth voice declared.

Khakhati looked at Neferure, who looked at Sahu, who then looked back and forth between the two cats in front of him. None of them had uttered a word. The voice they had heard sounded as if it were weathered by years of pain and struggle, far more years than any of them had lived. In unison the three of them turned towards the old cat, who was no longer fast asleep. Unlike his dull fur and dishevelled appearance, his eyes were full of life and wisdom.

'Who are you?' Sahu asked.

'I am Khu.'

An instant silence.

Neferure thought back to the first time Khakhati introduced himself, when he stated the names of the ancestors of his lineage. 'You're Khakhati's grandfather?' she asked. 'You're of Per-Maahes?'

'Yes, I am of that lineage.' His words were delivered slowly and carefully. 'Of that I was once proud.'

Khakhati's face was blank like an uncarved stone. Khu looked at him, momentarily sizing up his grandson, and then continued, moving straight to the heart of the matter.

'The weapon I shall give you is one of knowledge. You must know this: their leader is no ordinary stray. Mehen is my son.'

Khu closed his eyes. With great strain he continued speaking. 'There can be only one chosen per litter to uphold the lineage, or else none. Mehen was born with great potential, but on Maahes's request I initiated his sister, Djah, into the lineage. Maahes assured me that Mehen would understand. Mehen did not. That day he left

Abydos for Thebes, saying he would never forgive me. For many moons afterwards I tried to reconcile myself to this decision, though I could not. One day I left my amulet in the Nile and journeyed here, to Karnak, to watch over my son, though he does not know it. I gave up on Maahes's wisdom, and I gave up on my lineage.'

Neferure wondered how he was keeping an eye upon his son, but there was little time for such questions. 'Still, none of this helps explain how Akhotep's ankh is of use, nor the meaning of the river of light,' she said, figuring Khu had heard their whole conversation. 'Without that knowledge our quest is useless.'

Khu slowly and painfully curled his paws, folding them under his chest. He opened his bright eyes again and, with jerking movements, looked directly at Neferure. His breath rattled. 'Long have I been a follower of Thoth, as well as Maahes, and through the years I have come to understand the inner workings and subtleties of his wisdom. There is a place, a long-abandoned temple on the West Bank of Thebes, standing upon the highest peak of the necropolis. The temple was dedicated to Horus, although Thoth has often been contacted within its walls. The veil Apep has placed to shroud the god's view is thick. If there is anyone who can see through it, it will be him, the cleverest of all gods. Hopefully, he will shed light that is of use to you on your quest.'

Sahu would need to rob the tomb of the high priest he had betrayed while Neferure went across a desert to consult with a god. What if Thoth refused to speak with her? Neferure briefly considered that Takhaet might hold the right views on how to live life: lie around and be pampered.

Khakhati shook off his entrancement. 'I have heard many great things about my grandfather, and I refuse to accept that he would disown his heritage over one son who turned stray.'

A great strain came over Khu's face and he looked down at the polished temple floor as he spoke, continuing without addressing Khakhati's criticism. 'Certainly Mehen knew what gift Maahes had placed upon his path. You can imagine the pain it must have caused him when his grand future was revealed to be nothing more than a mirage. This is his form of rebellion, to take power without being given it. The strays now venerate him, and they would not if they knew his true lineage, for they have little respect for those who are esteemed among housecats. Knowledge of someone's past can be more powerful than the sharpest claw if one knows how to use it.'

'Why are you telling us this?' Neferure asked.

'Because your quest is more important than any single life, even my son's.'

'Wait,' Sahu said, drawing toward Khu. 'Khesef-hra mentioned placing a wax figure of Apep in the inner sanctum of Amun-Ra. He said it would be used for one of Apep's manifestations to rise.'

'You need not concern yourself with that,' Khu told him. 'Instead you must look at the bigger picture. You must render that tool, and any others of its kind, useless.' With that last sentence uttered, Khu's eyes closed once more, and his body collapsed back down onto the cold polished stone.

Sahu watched Khu's breathing sink into the steady

rhythm of sleep. 'How am I to enter Akhotep's tomb?' he asked Neferure.

Neferure was lost in thought, her minds still dwelling on all Khu had said and his unexpected awakening. Khakhati's posture slumped for the first time in Neferure's presence. Likely Khakhati was having a hard time coming to terms with knowing that the most decrepit cat he'd ever seen was the grandfather he had held in the highest esteem.

'A shaft should lead down into the burial chamber,' Sahu thought aloud, 'to allow Akhotep's spirit to return to his body. Hopefully the shaft will be wide enough for me to fit through.'

Khakhati's back tensed like a taut bow, his head snapped towards Sahu. 'It wasn't enough that you disgraced Akhotep in life, but now you want to rob his tomb? Have you no respect for the dead?'

Again Sahu flattened his ears. 'Not when the secrets affect the living.'

Neferure struck them both a look of disgust.

'Very well.' Khakhati's righted his posture. 'Your missions are set. I will guard your paths until you are out of Thebes, and then I will search for The Word.'

CHAPTER 13

The Strays

THE HOT BREATH of Sekhmet roared across the land. Each strong gust of wind spewed dust into the air. Neferure squinted and shook her fur clean. Sahu cautiously scanned their surroundings, and Khakhati strutted down the last stretch of street before the city turned into farmland.

'You'd better be sure about this.' Sahu gave a skeptical glance towards Khakhati, who kept several paces in front. 'I'm not any more welcome with the strays than I am with housecats. Deserters aren't welcome.'

'Trust me,' were the only two uninspiring words Khakhati gave as they passed through the line of sentinels at the edge of Thebes.

Several cats looked down from the rooftops, their faces blank at the sight of the unlikely trio. 'This matter will be explained in due course,' Khakhati said. 'Bring some of the guard to the grasses along the western border of the city. Have them wait for me there.'

Neferure wondered how Khakhati originally planned to deal with the strays before Khu told Mehen's life story. Likely it would have involved the skilled, but excessive, use of claws and teeth. She wasn't sure which plan she preferred. Being at the sole mercy of Khakhati's negotiating skills was not comforting. Still, it was possible that he was not working for the good of housecats alone, and she made a note to keep a close eye on his actions and words. Khakhati knew too much and was one of only two cats in Thebes who wore an amulet. Although no harm had befallen them in house cat territory, Neferure still did not place trust in him—especially since to do so would implicate her friend Ahmes.

Thebes now lay many paces behind them. Only a few plots of farmland served as a buffering zone between strays and housecats. The three travelled along a worn, narrow, earthen road. The fields were dry and dying. The wind had settled down; every blade of grass stood still. Far off to their left, the Nile ran steady and silent.

A hippopotamus broke through the water, ending the calm. The large creature ambled his way through the field and sat down in a patch of tall barley.

Halting the creation of a new water channel, the land-owner slowly turned, dreading what had happened. His eyes grew wide at what he saw sitting in the middle of his field. 'You're destroying my crops, you despicable, three-ton, profit-crushing animal!' he yelled. 'How am I supposed to pay my taxes now? I don't suppose you're going to pay them for me. Oh, if I had my hunting tools on hand...'

The hippopotamus twitched his ears and looked at the man with a vacant expression, then lay down.

'For the love of Amun, don't do that!' The landowner cradled his head in his hands.

Sahu turned to Neferure and gave a sly laugh.

Khakhati shot a glance of disgust back at Sahu, the first time he'd looked him in the eye since they had begun their journey. 'Only strays would have the callousness to find humour in the misfortune of others.'

A living shadow stepped before their path. 'We certainly would find humour in *your* misfortune.'

Neferure shrunk back onto her hindquarters. Her eyes were opened wide and glued to the strong and muscular cat who had just made his presence known. He was past his prime, but far from decrepit. The disorganized spot pattern on his coat blended smoothly with his dark, smoky grey fur, doing little to hide the numerous scars on his body. Copper-tipped hairs seemed as though they were caught in embers from a fire that refused to die. A number of cats stood behind him and others off to the side, silently watching from the fields. He glanced briefly at Khakhati's amulet, then intensely studied its bearer.

Looking into that stray's eyes, Neferure saw a struggle, a steely coldness hiding a stormy desert of pain and anger. 'Can you challenge him?' she whispered, turning toward Khakhati.

'Yes.' Khakhati's voice carried uncertainty. He then stepped forward with the slightest delay, tail rigid in the air. 'I am Khakhati of Per-Maahes, son of Djah, the daughter of—'

'We see the point,' the stray interrupted.

'I demand passage across the Nile for my companions.'

'Very well, Khakhati of Per-Maahes. First give me the time to introduce myself. I am Mehen, leader of the strays, and I do not defer to anyone. Now tell me, *housecat*, why do you wish to pass through our lands?'

Khakhati, always eager for a confrontation, did not flinch. Mehen had eyes that could burn holes through one's courage. Yet Khakhati had the command and bearing befitting a wearer of Maahes' amulet.

A lean cat with an unusually pointed face emerged from the field and unsheathed his claws. 'Why should we let you pass?' he asked. 'You who refuse to answer to the strays.'

Khakhati stepped forward and looked Mehen in the eyes. 'You didn't need to introduce yourself. I already know of you. And we both know what this amulet means.'

Mehen shifted some weight onto his back paws. Khakhati's hints had caught him off guard. However, Mehen was not one to back down.

At the flick of Mehen's tail, strays emerged from the fields and closed in around Neferure, Sahu, and Khakhati. Most had anger boiling in their eyes, a symptom of the plague that Neferure had felt manifesting in herself. Rustling grasses from all sides revealed far more cats surrounding them than Neferure had originally thought.

Sahu looked towards Mehen. 'Words can travel faster than claws.'

'True.' Mehen met Sahu's gaze. 'But their validation does not.'

'I have proof of what I know,' Khakhati said. '*He* who granted an amulet to Djah is still alive.'

Mehen's shoulders pressed backwards, and his tail stiffened. The strays halted their advance, curious to find out the meaning behind Khakhati's words.

'*He* knows where you are and that the three of us set out to meet you. *He* will know if we do not return, and if so will make known the secret you keep.' Khakhati diverted his glance to the strays. 'If they would leave, we could make an agreement.'

Mehen's eyes widened. His tail thrashed.

'I have nothing to hide. You've lingered here long enough, *housecats*.' Upon another flick of his tail the strays advanced.

Negotiations had failed. Neferure pressed her back against the grasses, glancing about, assessing all possible escape routes. A dreadful shadow veiled the land. A sickly halo of light surrounded a darkened sun, casting a pale and deathly glow upon Sahu's silver fur. Trembling grew in the ground, violently shifting the dirt beneath their paws. All the cats grew fearful. Some arched their backs, spitting at the air. The ocean of strays parted and ran for cover, their tails as wide as bushes.

Neferure shrunk closer to Sahu, fur standing on end, and looked at the shrouded sun. Images of her nightmare flashed before her mind's eye: a stone serpent reaching to the sky and devouring the light. Shivers slithered up her spine. 'Apep,' she said, looking towards no one, 'endeavours to swallow Ra's solar barque.'

'Go!' Khakhati launched himself at the lean cat, taking advantage of the confusion.

Sahu and Neferure sped off, leaving Khakhati surrounded and fighting off a large number of cats.

They ran not ten paces before Mehen collided, full force, with Sahu, sending him spinning to the ground. Sahu lay there like a limp toy, stunned.

Mehen let out a low and deep growl. 'Never again will you threaten me. Know this: you will never be safe from me, not even in the inner depths of Thebes.'

In the distance Neferure saw Khakhati bolt towards Thebes—drawing the strays into an inevitable housecat ambush.

Sahu collected himself, though he remained pressed low to the ground. He glared at Mehen, his voice stoic. 'Another who knows your secret is now heading towards Thebes. If Khakhati learns about our fate by your claws, your own future will be darker than this hour. You know very well the strays will not follow a highborn housecat posing as a rogue. If they learn you were almost initiated into the lineage of—'

'Pass quickly through these lands and speak not another word.' Mehen thrashed his tail and glared at them as they departed.

'I'm not sure we can fully trust him,' Neferure whispered once they were out of earshot. 'A stray threatened Heqaib from just outside of Karnak, and I'm certain that it was Mehen he described.'

'Karnak? Then we must remain vigilant, though we have no choice now but to continue.'

The further Neferure and Sahu walked along the earthen path, the more it broadened. Surrounding fields grew thicker and greener. The sun had begun to escape the grasp of darkness and now shone partially on the land. A single ray of light lit up the western hills, the horizon beyond which the dead passed when they journeyed to Amenti. The soil beneath their paws became darker and richer.

Beyond the final bend in the path lay the riverbank. In the distance a small, old wooden boat floated like a bug drowning in a pool of water, tied to shore by a worn rope fastened to a rotten stake of wood. Dwarfed by the massive and powerful Nile, it seemed as undependable as the bones of the thin, elderly man who hobbled across the deck, mending tattered sails.

Sahu and Neferure paused. Treading through a marsh was one thing, and it was an unpleasant one at that. Swimming towards a rickety boat attached to no dock at all was quite another.

'When we agreed to try to defeat Apep,' Sahu said, 'we both knew there would be danger and life-threatening challenges, but no one said *anything* about getting wet.'

Neferure remained silent. She stared with an open mouth at the boat that seemed to defy all laws enabling objects to float. The next voices to be heard came from deep within the field and off to their left.

'Why were Sahu and that highly preened housecat offered free passage through lands which are no longer his?' said a harsh and snappy voice. 'I despise seeing his paws on our soil. As soon as Sahu stepped back onto our lands, the sun grew dark.'

Neferure recognized the voice. It was that of the lean cat with the unusually pointed face, the one who had chided Khakhati for ignoring Mehen. Quickly and stealthily she and Sahu moved on. As they made their way down the path, they spoke not a word to each other, listening solely to the muffled conversation in the fields. The rustling of leaves made it obvious the strays were stalking them.

'For what reason,' asked another voice from within the field, 'are we now treating the housecats with more respect than they have given us?'

Gradually, Sahu and Neferure sped up, soundlessly treading down the path towards the small wooden boat. The rustling noises first kept pace, then quickened, hastening their way to the river's bank.

'Because Mehen is hiding something important,' the snappy voice replied. 'We've trusted him until now, but we cannot trust him any further. Those who still do shall face our wrath. A cat with greater skill than Mehen ever had—Lufni the Great—will now guard these lands. No, Lufni the Conqueror! I will start by ridding our territory of all housecats and betrayers. If left to their own devices, Sahu and his housecat friend will surely be dead before the sun sets on the West Bank. Why don't we quicken their end?'

Neferure and Sahu glanced at each other. Their eyes both lit as if a current of thought had jolted through their minds. Simultaneously they darted towards the boat.

The lean cat with the pointed face stepped out before their path just as Mehen had done earlier. A large group of strays came and flanked him on both sides. Sahu and Neferure skidded to a halt.

'Mehen has let you pass,' the pointy-faced stray declared, 'but we shall not.'

CHAPTER 14

Across the Nile

ANGER SHOT THROUGH Neferure's veins as suddenly and strongly as the venomous bite of an asp.

She wrinkled her nose at the blockade of strays and found herself quoting Takhaet. 'Your wretched hearts have angered the gods.' She hissed. 'You live in chaos and disease because every day you deviate from the philosophies of Ma'at. You have been ousted by the gods, and so you have been ousted by the housecats.'

Sahu glanced apprehensively at her.

The pointy-faced stray turned his head in one sharp and direct movement. 'Housecats are to blame for the plague. You took our lands street by street until we no longer had even the city's edge as our territory. How are we to be well when forced to live off plague bearing mice? Soon we will regain what lands we have lost, and more.' He trotted up the pathway, flanked by the remaining strays. 'Soon the privileges afforded to housecats will again be available to us. Yours will be the first blood to be spilt in a prelude to our new beginning.'

'Well, this is why we must always have a backup plan.'

Sahu said, watching the formation of strays advance, their heads lowered, their tails stiff and arched.

'Split up,' Neferure whispered. 'We'll lose them in the fields. Make a wide semicircle and then head straight for the boat.'

'I thought it was my job to get us both killed.'

'Go!'

With their sharp claws scraping through the rich soil, Neferure and Sahu darted into the fields, each taking an opposite direction. Fleet of foot, Neferure dashed through the barley grasses, aware of every small detail, every stone she ran over and every plant stalk that brushed against her fur. She circled long and wide, leading the strays far from the boat, hoping she could lose sight of them.

When all noise of pursuit came solely from behind, Neferure changed directions, dashing towards the west, towards the Nile.

Rapidly she gained distance from the strays, who could follow her only by sound. Every change of direction she made took them seconds longer to recognize. Surely a few strays had run back to block passage to the boat—though at least she and Sahu would stand a fighting chance against them. Before long they would be safely on board.

Neferure skidded to a halt. Before her immediate path ran a newly created irrigation channel. The channel was deep and wide. Although still dry, it was not to remain that way for long.

Having just completed his long and tedious labour, the landowner smiled, looked back at his proud work, and then shovelled aside the remainder of the dirt that held back water stored from the previous flood. From the south the floodwater came surging down the channel. Neferure calculated her jump. She crouched down, ready to unleash the latent power in her muscles and spring to the opposite bank.

Out of the grasses from behind leapt the pointy-faced stray—paws outstretched, claws unsheathed.

Neferure slid to the side and watched her opponent crash face first to the ground.

The plague was kindling in the eyes of the pointy-faced stray. He was affected enough by his sickness to have increased anger but not yet enough to have impaired movement, thus making him a deadly adversary.

Any chance to cross the irrigation channel had been lost. Emerald green water swiftly rushed by. What looked like a large and lumpy log surfed upon the waves, speaking in a deep voice.

'I've got a bad case of gravity,' it moaned dejectedly. 'Nature's working against me again. Why does everything work against me? Why am I always the outcast?'

As Neferure's eyes focused, the log morphed into a crocodile. Caught in the heat of battle, the pointy-faced stray noticed nothing unusual. He leapt again.

A heavy weight impacted Neferure from her side, rolling her over onto the dark earth. Her skin was grazed by many sharp claws, one of which dug too deep. A sharp yowl flew through her throat and into the air.

Unlike her first fight with the strays, Neferure was now mentally prepared. She attacked rather than only defending, biting her opponent in the neck as she had seen

Khakhati do. Her deflections of strikes came swiftly and confidently. Still, she was losing the battle.

Inch by inch, Neferure was pushed toward the edge of the deep irrigation channel. Through the wisps of fur and claw she could see the two round eyes of a crocodile watching the battle despondently.

One of Neferure's back paws slid down the short bank and dipped into the water. The crocodile silently moved closer and separated his jaws. Frantically Neferure swatted at the eyes of her opponent and won enough time to regain her footing.

For a breath's length the battle paused.

Both adversaries circled the other, their heads pressed against their hunched backs. Their hackles were raised, and their tails were puffed and erect.

Dancing on her tiptoes, Neferure sidestepped through the grasses. She squinted as she broke through veils of plant leaves. She paused and watched her opponent, looking out behind a tattered green curtain. From side to side her tail swished; now lowered to the ground.

Neferure leapt. Her paws pointed forward, raised as a guard against her face, protecting her as she landed squarely upon the back of the pointy-faced stray, pushing him to the ground. She bit him hard in the neck purely out of revenge. In an automatic reaction, his back paws threw her aside. Neferure landed on the ground, rolled over onto her back and assumed a defensive posture, her paws in the air, protecting her stomach and head.

His was a difficult guard to break, and so the pointy-faced stray paused, with his back to the irrigation channel, calculating his next move.

Movement in the water caught Neferure's eye. She averted her gaze, and so did her opponent once he saw the look of fear in her eyes.

A mouth full of crooked teeth arose from the water and engulfed the pointy-faced stray.

Exhilarated, the goofy looking crocodile began rolling around in the water, eating his prey. Lufni the Conquerer's short reign had been ended by a most unlikely source—a depressed crocodile.

Neferure swivelled her right ear backwards and caught the sounds of a hurried pursuit. More strays were on their way. She rallied her courage and calculated her jump. Drawing on latent energy she sprung onto the crocodile's back, propelling towards the opposite bank. Her paws touched solid ground the instant more strays broke through the grasses. None were willing to follow her daring escape.

'I'm on a mission to cure the plague,' she turned around and hissed. 'Now I wish I could selectively cure housecats.' *At least housecats don't try to kill those who can help them*, Neferure thought. Then she recalled their intentions for Sahu.

The boat. That was her focus. Neferure disappeared fast into the fields.

She met up with Sahu upon the last stretch of pathway before the Nile. His fur was drenched. A few small scratches marred his skin, but nothing serious like her previous bite wound.

'I see one of us managed to escape from an unwanted bath.'

Neferure laughed. She almost felt back to the carefree days before Akhotep's death. 'I simply seized an advantageous moment.'

Sahu looked toward the five strays still standing between them and their passage to the West Bank. 'Let's hope advantage remains on our side.'

The old man was untying the dilapidated rope holding his boat to the shore. He was having some trouble with the unnecessarily complicated knot he had made. In his attempts to unravel the rope, it broke at its weakest point. The old man cursed under his breath and drew the rest of the line back onto the deck. He then picked up a heavily dented farmer's shovel instead of an oar and began pushing the small boat away from the shoreline.

Neferure scanned the bank for crocodiles. She found none. 'We have to hurry!'

'Just swim around those wretched cats!' Sahu said. 'I've had enough of their madness.'

Again Sahu and Neferure diverged. Sahu, already wet, dove readily into the Nile. Neferure paused for a second at the water's edge, diving in only to escape fast moving claws.

Water did not stop the strays. All five followed in a fiery pursuit, biting and snapping at what scrap of fur and tail they could reach, getting mostly mouthfuls of slimy green water.

The old man began to raise the sail. Neferure and Sahu were but inches away from the boat. They dug their claws into the rough wood on the stern, as did one relentless stray. Wind gathered in the square sail and drove the boat through the water. The three cats clung on as they were dragged through the Nile, clambering slowly up the slippery and splintered wood.

Sahu yowled in sudden pain. Hanging on with one paw, he turned and swatted the stray whose teeth had clamped down upon his tail. The stray released his bite and lost his hold on the boat. He fell back into the water, grasping again for a foothold, finding one.

Neferure and Sahu drew their sopping wet bodies onto the deck, the stray only feet behind.

The old man's eyes lit up. Realizing something was not quite right, he grabbed his shovel in his hands and walked across the deck. 'Sorry!' he yelled as he swept the stray off the side of his boat with the farming tool, dumping him unceremoniously into the Nile. 'I only let two little furry wonders on board at a time.'

For a good while, no one moved. The old man stared at the two soaked cats catching their breaths after their unrelenting struggle to board his boat.

Sahu looked at Neferure's recent wound and her laboured breathing. Her lungs and chest were tight with anger. Her eyes were carefully avoiding the bright setting sun and her pupils seemed more dilated than they should have been. 'Is there anything you want to tell me?' he asked cautiously.

Neferure said nothing. She could not tell Sahu about her fears of the plague or how the light now stung her eyes. Sahu needed to concentrate on their goal, not on uncertain worry. In any case, she was perfectly fine.

A gust of wind blew from the north and rocked the boat from side to side. Neferure's tail dipped into the water.

Anxiously, she dug every single claw deep into the wood and dared not look back.

The old man chuckled. 'Hitching a free ride so you don't have to swim. Yes, I know your species has no great love for water. Isn't it funny how cats drink what they fear?' He paused to study the horizon, tilting his head to one side. 'No, it's probably not funny.' He let out a deep breath. 'Oh hi ho.'

Neferure remembered hearing that humans often paid the old man more than their full fare just for him to keep quiet. Unfortunately she was not afforded that privilege.

'Bet you didn't know that back in my day I was going to become pharaoh,' the old man said.

Neferure and Sahu looked at each other. The ride was sure to be very long.

Tattered ends of the large sail flapped in the wind. The old man looked towards the setting sun, watching the ripples in the Nile sparkle like drops of liquid gold. While he continued his life's story, he did not take his eyes off the rocky Theban hills that guarded the horizon. 'Yes,' he muttered, 'I had it all planned out. I was going to build the first ever inverted pyramid. That would show everyone who was boss. The pharaohs of today just aren't as they used to be. I still remember when Ramesses II defeated that old sea monster using only words and intimidation. He didn't need any weapons.' The old man chuckled. 'Or shovels for that matter.'

'Sea monster?' Sahu questioned.

'Exactly how many years ago did Ramesses II reign?' Neferure asked.

'I don't know,' Sahu said, 'but I do know that I'm more afraid here than I was in stray territory.'

The old man continued, as if hearing Neferure's question. 'I know what you're probably thinking. How could this man have been alive during the reign of Ramesses II when we're already on our third Ramesses? Well, it happened to be that I was mistaken for dead because I choked on a leek. My family was quick to go ahead with the burial procedure; didn't even bother to have me properly mummified—or check if I yet breathed. They figured that since I stopped talking I must be dead. They wrapped me up and stuck me in some random cave. I slept quite a while. I slept past the reign of, say, five pharaohs ... until some children started poking me with sticks. They were shown a thing or two.

'Speaking of which, some no good youths tried to break into the tomb that high priest was recently buried in.' The old man shook his head. 'No respect. The dead get no respect these days.'

Sahu's eyes lit up and his ears perked. 'If they stole the ankh…'

'Now, kitties,' the old man said as he noticed the boat was approaching the West Bank, 'I'm going to let you in on a secret. I've had strange dreams. Dreams about a future where stories are told about me and my fake death. These stories are meant to frighten people into not waking the dead. In my dreams they call me a "mummy".'

'I can't believe the strays guard the passage to this boat,' Neferure said.

'This man gets stranger and stranger,' Sahu replied.

'Ah, here we are.' The old man smiled as the boat approached a small wooden dock. No longer having any rope, he extended a wooden board from the deck to the dock. 'So long, kitties.' He gave one quivering wave. 'Remember to keep a good distance away from the future, and never forget that I'm the original mummy.'

'We'll try to forget,' Sahu said, 'but don't worry, I doubt we'll succeed.'

Together they set foot upon the West Bank, the realm of the dead. A different atmosphere permeated that land, as if the barrier of time had no meaning and the silence held a thousand stories, each whispering their secrets upon the wind. Not death, but rather eternal life saturated those soils.

Neferure looked towards the peak of the Theban necropolis. The high pyramid-shaped hill stood, overlooking the Valley of the Kings.

Sahu nuzzled her. 'This is where our paths split.'

A purr gathered in Neferure's throat. 'Promise me we will see each other again in this life.'

'I promised I would not leave you on this earth alone.'

Rays from the setting sun pushed their shadows across the land. Neferure gave one quick lick to Sahu's forehead before she tore towards the barren hills. She knew he watched her as she ran, leaving paw prints in the soft irrigated earth. Then he turned to his own path, to the tomb he'd once evaded.

CHAPTER 15

House of Eternity

THE SUNSET ENDED in a clash of colour, leaving behind a clear starlit sky. Sahu sped across the desert, travelling the most recent scent trail of human feet and incense, towards Akhotep's tomb. The winds mercilessly blew upon the West Bank, sweeping across the barren landscape, voices of the dead lending to the desert's rage. He could see little beyond his immediate path, and his fur was soaked in rough sand granules.

Grass and rock were the only dependable scent indicators to help Sahu follow the path of the funeral procession. He fought against wind and sand, purposefully edging his way forward, glad only for the night's refuge from Amun's radiant heat.

This would have been much easier if I were carried there along with the rest of the cats, Sahu morbidly thought. Perhaps there would have been no funeral at all, had he done his duty and warned Akhotep of the fires. *No*, he reminded himself, *none of the other cats were able to wake him. I could not have helped.* He put more speed into his stride.

In the far distance loomed Hatshepsut's mortuary temple, cradled by the Theban hills. Beyond that rise, in the Valley of the Kings, lay many of Egypt's most splendid tombs. Pharaohs—some the greatest who had ever ruled—lay eternally beneath layers of rock, buried with their lordly treasures. Painted on the walls of their tombs were images of their dearest relations, great gods, and depictions of the path their souls would follow to safely pass the trials of Amenti.

Veiled in clouds of dust stood a lone desert tree blistered by the sun's fire and dying slowly under the moonlight. Its roots were shrivelling under the ground, its leaves turning to dust and falling upon the sands, its branches crumbling to ash.

The raging winds ran out of breath. Curtains of sand parted to reveal the entrance into the high priest's tomb.

Akhotep's eternal house was carved out of rock at the very base of the Theban hillside. A stone frame held the splintered remains of a thick wooden door. Sahu was reminded much of the ruins that filled his first memories. The day he was born had been the day he became a stray—all because of one collapsed house.

Spanning the whole width of the doorway was an intricate and delicate net of woven silk, capturing both starlight and dying breaths. None ever returned from that realm of beauty and deceit. In the centre lay a large, long legged spider. The creature waited among ribbons of moonlight, floating upon midnight air for a chance to perform its deadly dance—a play of light and shadow.

An unsettled feeling lurked at the back of his mind, slithering further away each time he reached to grasp its meaning. Taking a single deep breath he continued onwards, sliding into the tomb as fluidly as the uneasy feeling slipped through his thoughts.

A short stairway led down into the subterranean abyss where Akhotep rested. There were only two rooms: a long, horizontal vestibule and a burial chamber just beyond. The light of the waning moon reached only to the end of the vestibule, leaving the room with Akhotep's mummified body in darkness.

The tomb showed evidence of a hurried robbery. Many of Akhotep's prized possessions lay scattered on the floor. Sahu took care not to tread upon anything. He tested each step with his highly tactile paw pads before placing down his full weight. The last beam of pale moonlight spilled upon a small stone sarcophagus that had been hastily tipped over. Sahu realized at once what it had contained. He crouched down and scanned the surrounding area with his nose and whiskers. The air reeked of death. Several mummified cats were strewn upon the ground.

In life they had been his friends. He recalled lazy days spent by the sacred lake, Khaemwaset's boastful tales, Djaty absconding with Akhotep's dinner of Nile perch, Behenu vouching for him to become a temple cat…

No one was here to protect their mummies as they tried to protect Akhotep, Sahu thought as he stared directly at a death that would have been his. Shame washed over him as he continued on to raid the tomb.

Sahu reached the end of the vestibule and passed through a short corridor. The last remnants of light vanished as he entered Akhotep's burial chamber. Even Sahu's acute feline eyes could not see much through the murkiness of the chamber. Only his whiskers and nose could gather information about his surroundings. He couldn't tell how big the room was, where Akhotep's sarcophagus lay or, more importantly, where the ankh had been placed.

Somewhere in the roof above was a shaft leading to the stars—Sahu's original plan to enter the tomb, but its location no longer held relevance. His sole mission was to find the ankh.

Festering worries trailed down from his thoughts and into his heart, taking root in his mind's eye as lethal shadows creeping and crawling amongst the funerary items.

Sahu pressed further into the burial chamber. The room was much more cluttered than the vestibule. His whiskers navigated him past furniture, chests and jars. Akhotep's ankh could be anywhere. Phantom fears attacked Sahu from all angles, vanishing before impact. He walked on only to escape them. They matched pace. He crashed into a large golden chest. Breaths quickened.

An entity was with him in the tomb. He could feel it. Someone or something meant him harm.

An alabaster jar toppled and fell, shattering against the rough stone. Fleetingly, Sahu jumped to the side. Instead of touching stone, one of his front paws landed upon a smooth metallic surface with delicate engravings—a piece of jewellery. His heart beat faster, then skipped for one long beat.

'Traitor.'

A voice, feminine and deadly, rattled down the star shaft. Sahu tensed. He scanned for its source. The tomb was drenched in silence.

'*This crime will not go unpunished.*'

From the star shaft a cobra dropped, its serpentine body thudding onto the floor. She slithered forwards, scales upon stone, swimming in the ocean of darkness. A waft of air slid over Sahu's front paws. Meretseger, the guardian of the dead, had sent an assailant for him.

'*Betrayer of the dead,*' the voice sounded again from all angles of the tomb, '*your judgement awaits.*'

CHAPTER 16

Thoth

CULTIVATED LAND SLOWLY turned into savannah, and savannah into desert. Green burned to gold under the sun's fading rays as Neferure followed the narrow path leading to the peak of the Theban necropolis. She trudged over sharp rocks and stones on the final stretch of her journey. Just as Khu said, the small temple loomed above her, before the twilight sky.

The Valley of the Kings hid directly below at the bottom of the steep rock face, guarded by both men and a deadly goddess, swallowing up the dark shades of night. Wafts of cold, ghostly air rose from those depths and combed through Neferure's fur, bringing sudden chills to her skin.

Hatshepsut, Thutmose III, Ramesses the Great, and his father Seti I—among many of Egypt's greatest pharaohs— lay buried beneath dirt, rock, and memory. Their names were still spoken in the streets of Egypt, and their statues stood forever before the temples, though they walked now only in Amenti. They had built grand effigies to the gods, and in return they had been rewarded with immortality among both the living and the dead.

Neferure's nightmare resurfaced from the recesses of her mind and brought back the image of shattered statues—broken, forgotten, and lying in the shadow cast by a stone serpent. Did the prevention of that future, she wondered, really all depend on what information would be given to her within the walls of a dilapidated and forgotten temple?

She hoped Thoth would tell her everything she needed to hear. She wanted desperately for him to become the voice in the darkness that Amun-Ra had not been—the voice that would answer her questions.

Nothing truly made her believe Thoth would answer her any more readily than Amun-Ra. With desperation and hopelessness she made her journey, not with faith or certainty. Her once insatiable curiosity towards the unknown had flown away in the talons of a vulture.

Pulling herself over a large boulder, Neferure's steep and tiring climb ended at last. The temple was so close that even its small size blocked out most of the night sky. Dark, small and ominous, its doorway seemed more like the entrance to the tomb Sahu was breaking into rather than the house of a god.

She stopped before the doorway and ascertained its safety. Her ears were alert, her muscles lithe and filled with raw harnessed power. She was ready to bolt at the slightest sign of danger.

One cautious step at a time, she walked in, setting her tired paws upon ancient stone. Eyes adjusted to the darkened interior, and she noticed there were no writings or images on the walls of the small room. Directly in front lay the inner sanctum.

She paused outside and gazed into its stark and empty space. The whole temple seemed no different from an abandoned house that had outlived its use.

Neferure knew not what to do. How was she to initiate contact with Thoth?

Simply ask, she thought, responding to her own question. Words formed in her mind, giving her speech she felt did not come from her own memory.

'Rise to meet me, Thoth, great of wisdom who dwells in the halls of Amenti. Rise from the earth, Thoth, and have your spirit fill this sanctum.'

A presence hung over Neferure's shoulder. She glanced backwards and saw only stone framing a dark and glittering sky. Looking back at the inner sanctum it seemed different. Now an ancient power inhabited its walls. Something took breath in the darkness and filled the room with life. To step inside would be to disturb the past. The walls themselves felt now as though they were sealed with ancient words from a time when the hearts of gods walked along the Nile, when Osiris himself lived and ruled over Egypt.

Neferure stepped in.

A voice, long forgotten in the land of Egypt, lost in the echoes of time, filled the temple. It filled the space like an enormous living being, and every word resounded with power and an inherent impression of truth and wisdom. 'Hear me. I am Thoth, and I have heeded your request. Few make the effort needed to seek me out, and you are to be commended for your faith.'

'*My faith?*' Neferure asked. 'No, it was desperation that brought me here. I need answers to powerful questions.'

She did not expect Thoth to offer much in the way of aid. Perhaps he would leave now that he knew she wished for more than to offer praise.

'Ask,' Thoth replied, 'and an answer shall be given.'

Surprised and caught off guard by his willingness, Neferure found herself posing a completely different question than she had come to ask. Information about the use of Akhotep's ankh had been her priority and purpose. At that moment it did not seem relevant.

'Every day,' she said, 'just before sunrise, I see a river of light, heading towards me and the land. It flows beyond the vision of all others, yet it completely clouds my senses. The force of it is growing stronger. I must know how to stop this from happening.'

'The river of light is the energy of the star Sopdet, the star of Isis,' the voice of Thoth replied methodically. 'As the Opening of the Year draws closer and Sopdet readies to rise, the energy, the river of light that you see, grows. Neferure, you must understand that your connection to this star is your power. Do not shun it.'

Neferure wrinkled her nose. 'I don't understand how any good can come of this "power".'

Swirls of light manifested in the air and formed into the vague shape of large ibis wings. Thoth flew down from above, briefly encapsulating Neferure in light. Regally he landed where once there had been an altar. Like wisps of cloud blown by wind, the blue light pulsated and dimmed, forming an ever-changing outline of the great god of mysteries. The air cooled, and Neferure's fur stood on end. Thoth's voice now emanated from his luminescent form.

'A boat sails only by wind,' he declared. 'When there is no wind, there is no motion, no progress for the boat. None can see the wind, yet it can sail them to new horizons. The strongest forces often go unseen and unrealized, such as the energies of the stars, of the heavens.'

'How am I to use this force?' Neferure asked, pressing for answers, fearing she would not learn enough before Thoth left.

'Use this power to defeat Apep.'

'You know of my quest?'

'Many of the gods are watching you closely. Though, our view of the moral realm has been clouded as of late.' Thoth stretched his wide majestic wings to the temple roof. 'Apep is a power even we have difficulty restraining. The light of Sopdet will impede his rising, but it cannot stop him entirely. You must use Akhotep's ankh upon Apep's altar to focus these energies. Think of yourself as a star upon the earth and the light will be drawn to you. The forbidden temple must be destroyed to prevent Apep's rising and his influence from seeping through the sands of Egypt. You are one of the few who has the power to do this.'

For a while the god of magic and science was silent. His gaze pierced through the walls of the temple, watching some far off events unfold. One of his luminescent eyes widened ever so slightly.

'Please,' Neferure asked, 'tell me about this danger.'

Thoth looked directly at Neferure. 'Apep has power over many of the gods. His words are used as a weapon to twist your mind so it no longer trusts your heart. From there the god of chaos works to use your most primal instincts, such as fear and the hunger for power, to serve his own purposes and agendas. Consider no word Apep says to be true, no matter how much sense it seems to make to your mind. When you face him, be sure not to look into—'

A sharp pain pierced Neferure's front leg as if a cobra had bitten it. She fell to the stone floor, bathed in phantom agony. She did not hear the rest of Thoth's words; she was barely aware of the great wing beats above pressing down the cold air, exiting the temple and leaving the bare room lifeless once again.

'Thoth! Don't leave me,' she cried as she came to her senses. 'What was it I needed to know? Tell me!'

Her eyes scrambled throughout the lifeless inner sanctum. The walls seemed to constrict around her, stealing each shallow breath. 'Can the gods not repeat their own words?' she whispered faintly.

Something terrible must have happened. Every nerve in her body told her this was so. Neferure worked hard to convince herself otherwise. *Sahu must simply be stuck in the tomb*, she told herself. Then why had her leg burned like a snakebite? *Yes, Sahu was stuck in Akhotep's tomb.*

Neferure then recalled one more part in her nightmare: the part where the skeleton of a cat lay before an open tomb, encircled by a cobra.

CHAPTER 17

Guardian of the Dead

BREATHS BECAME HARDER to draw as lungs turned to lead. Lingering beyond sight, Meretseger's messenger waited. Drawn by the heat of Sahu's body, she knew his every move. Terror pumped through his veins. His nerves prickled with energy, waiting for orders.

Sahu considered his limited choices. He could either run from his barely visible attacker or fight any shadow that moved. All he needed was enough time to lay the ankh upon the sands outside the tomb. Neferure would come eventually, and in the open she ran less chance of being bitten herself.

Did Meretseger not know that Sahu's betrayal of Akhotep was ultimately for the good of Amun-Ra and all those who followed him? Likely not. Meretseger excelled at one thing: protecting the dead. She was eager to show her skill.

The moon, Thoth's eye, travelled in the sky. Its beams of pale light spread across the vestibule, spilling down the corridor and hitting the back of the burial chamber.

A river of darkness slithered through a stream of light.

Sahu looked around, scrambling to find escape. The spider's web at the tomb's entrance formed a net of shadow on the back wall, overlaid upon a painting of Akhotep greeting Osiris. To his left, Sahu could make out the vague shape of a sarcophagus. Above the sarcophagus, on the roof, was a single square a few shades darker than the rest. It could only be the star shaft, and the opening looked large enough for him to squeeze through.

With his paw pads, Sahu traced the shape of the jewellery he was standing upon, verifying that it was indeed Akhotep's ankh. He crouched down and grasped the circular end in his mouth, then sprang onto the lid of the sarcophagus. Two sharp fangs grazed the bottom of a rear paw as he was flying through the air.

Sahu landed smoothly upon the heavy stone lid, beneath which lay Akhotep's mummified and gold draped body.

'*Traitor*,' the cobra hissed, her voice booming louder than before. '*You cannot escape your doom.*'

I can try, Sahu thought, judging the distance between himself and the opening of the star shaft. He swivelled his ears, listening to the slithering noises encircling the sarcophagus. Occasionally the cobra paused, and Sahu could hear her tongue flicker beneath him, tasting his fear.

Sahu clamped his mouth down on the ankh. In one powerful vertical leap, he sprang towards the stars, travelling the same symbolic path meant for Akhotep's spirit. His front paws shot out on either side, bracing him in mid-air, his rear paws still dangling in the tomb.

Paw by paw, Sahu tried to shimmy upwards. The stone was fairly rough and provided some traction, but the effort required enormous strength. One paw pressed down upon a smooth patch of stone. He lost his footing and fell.

In mid-air Sahu twisted, landing firmly again upon Akhotep's sarcophagus, the ankh still in his mouth.

A dark shape rushed forwards. Fangs glinted in the murky light. Sahu jumped backwards, swatting at the cobra and hitting her upon the head.

Hind feet met only air. He slid off the edge of the thick stone lid, landing inside a tall alabaster jar. Metal clanked against stone. The ankh had fallen from his mouth. He pressed his paws against one side of the jar, tipping it over so the cobra could not follow. A crack travelled down the side, but the jar did not shatter. *Does Akhotep truly need all this clutter?* Sahu thought bitterly.

'*Even in your mind you betray the dead priest,*' the cobra hissed, her voice coming from the air itself.

Every strand of Sahu's fur stood on end, and his tail bushed out. He bolted out of the alabaster jar, realizing it was more a prison than a hideout. With his whiskers and paws, he searched the ground for the ankh.

The cobra dropped onto the floor and slid towards her prey. Meretseger's messenger of death met Sahu face to face. She reared up and spread her hood. Her fangs glistened with poison. Between him and certain death the ankh glimmered. Adrenaline replaced blood. His heart pounded against his chest as if it had been buried alive.

'*One who has obeyed Ma'at does not fear death as you do now,*' the cobra spat. Her head sailed forward like an arrow released from a bowstring.

Sahu jumped backwards into the side of the sarcophagus,

narrowly avoiding death. Meretseger's messenger advanced, slithering forward. For a few seconds her whole body touched the floor, enabling her strikes only to come from ground level. Sahu leapt over-top of her, grabbed the ankh and again sought the safety given by the height of the sarcophagus. His paws felt the wind off another fanged assault.

Sahu hurriedly calculated what might be his last leap and his last chance to live. He glanced back towards the tomb entrance. Too many of Akhotep's possessions were preventing a speedy escape. The star shaft was his only hope.

'Bast,' Sahu pleaded aloud, his voice muffled by the metal in his mouth 'please give me the strength to make this jump.'

'*Bast cannot help you.*' The cobra slithered up the side of the stone sarcophagus like shadowy water over a smooth rock. '*Your vain attempts to prolong your life in this world have ended any possibilities for the next.*' She levelled out upon the stone, then struck. As Sahu vaulted upwards, the serpent's sharp fangs reached to the stars.

All four of Sahu's paws braced him against stone. He'd succeeded.

Slowly and carefully he crawled his way up the shaft.

The shaft opening was covered with rubble, save for a small gap. An opening would need to be pawed out. Rocks and sand fell upon Sahu's face and back as he worked, tumbling towards the darkness he was seeking to escape.

Sahu tore out of the tomb as though emerging from a nightmare, his pulse racing. One deep breath of free night air marked his success. Meretseger had been outdone. Against all odds, he'd just outsmarted a goddess. He was unconquerable, more than ready to tackle any evil, including the serpent Apep. This was surely how Amun-Ra felt every time he safely made it through the underworld.

A speck of gold approached from the south. Sahu's ears and whiskers perked forward. He dropped the ankh upon the sand. His and Neferure's paths would indeed meet again.

In his mind Sahu began wording the tale of his escape, perfecting it to tell her. He started by omitting the part where he fell into the alabaster jar.

'You're alive!' Neferure shouted as she ran, tearing through the sand. 'I feared something terrible had happened.'

'On the contrary—I just escaped Meretseger! I escaped the Guardian of the Dead herself!'

Neferure's eyes glanced at the ankh. She brushed against Sahu, purring loudly. Then she looked toward the tomb and froze.

Sahu spun around. His body turned to ice.

The cobra hissed and spat at Sahu's face, then struck. Fangs pierced his leg, and poison shot into his veins. Death mingled with his blood, carrying the poison throughout his small body. Solid ground turned to waves. A dance of death played before Sahu's eyes as the fire of his life burned dim. Sahu stumbled and fell.

Neferure watched in horror.

'Have you found how to use the ankh?' he asked, gasping for air, his lungs rapidly paralysing. The cobra slithered away.

'Yes,' Neferure said, 'now let's go. Come on. Sahu! Walk!'

'I'm sorry. I have to break my promise. I can't stay here with you.'

Neferure lay down in the sands beside Sahu, her ears and whiskers both flattened. 'I don't know how I'm supposed to keep my promise either. This was not supposed to happen. I cannot let you be swallowed by darkness, but I cannot stop it either. Run Sahu, run from the gods. Do not let them judge you. *Please*.'

Words could not stop death. The promise they'd held between them was no more than an expression of hope. That single thought passed between them in their last moment together.

Sahu's eyes drew shut, and he took his final breath.

CHAPTER 18

The Weight of a Feather

DEATH SEEPED THROUGH the ground as Neferure's world spun out of orbit. She nuzzled Sahu's body. It grew cold beneath her nose. She could not bear to leave him, though she knew Sahu had already left her for Amenti—truly, this time.

Hours passed, and time did not drag away her pain. Despair pinned her to the earth. The dark sands sapped all of Neferure's warmth. Snake tracks led away from Sahu's body and over the ankh, the piece of jewellery he had died to uncover. Must she still complete her mission? Did it matter anymore? In time everyone must die and journey towards Amenti. She now looked forward to this journey.

Yet the land of the dead was not free from the threat of Apep. Sahu was still in danger. If the god of chaos learnt the secret name of Amun-Ra, he could destroy any lands his most hated enemy sailed past, including Amenti.

A new surge of energy and purpose rushed through Neferure. She would defeat Apep to save the lands of the dead—to save Sahu in the only way she yet could.

Again she glanced at the ankh. Now she feared neither

death nor any worldly danger. Into the desert Neferure set off, this time with an ankh and with no doubt that she and Sahu would be reunited in the afterworld. He would pass the weighing of the heart ceremony. Yes, her promise would have ensured that ... somehow.

Dull moonlight lit Neferure's path. Sand grabbed at her paws and the wind fought against her. Relentlessly she trod through desert and farmland bordering the Nile. All too slowly she came upon her destination.

A jackal howled in the distance: an eerie sound, as if summoning the dead to rise. She looked towards the boat for safety.

The old man had his back turned and was busy mending an old patched sail. Neferure crept her way onto the boat, not wanting to hear one more long-winded tale. Her attempt was in vain. The old man had an almost psychic connection to what transpired on his deck. He turned and looked around until his eyes caught sight of Neferure. The ankh was hidden behind her in a small nook.

'Oh! Kitty!' he exclaimed. Her very presence seemed to take ten years off his face. 'Look here. I've got something to show you.' He picked up a dilapidated rope. 'I had two bad ropes which I was able to tie together to make one good rope.' He held his knotted and worn-down scrap in front of her for a moment before throwing it into an assorted pile of other old and repurposed odds and ends. 'Who knows when it'll come in handy?'

From then on Neferure worked to ignore everything the old man said. What she may have found mildly amusing earlier now irritated her more than a conversation with

Takhaet. The old man picked up his digging tool, now even more battered and dented than before, and began retelling tales of how he'd spent the past hours. She looked away, setting her sights on Thebes.

'...and that's why I don't quite trust spells to keep nasty crocodiles away. Everybody uses those spells and magical rites, but I prefer my trusty old digging tool.'

Neferure had seen humans shed tears to rid themselves of sorrow. She now wished she could do the same.

She looked up at the waning moon. Pain shot through her eyes, and she lowered them to the deck, flattening her ears in the process. Her muscles trembled. All fear she had over Sahu's fate boiled to anger. At that moment she hated him for dying so suddenly after re-entering her life. Her breaths shortened, and her bite wound throbbed.

Emotional distress had caused her disease to quicken. *Why?! Why did Thoth not warn me about the plague?*

_____

Sahu opened his eyes. The deadly bite Meretseger's messenger had inflicted no longer burned in his leg. He glanced at the wound, expecting to see it fully healed. It was not. Instead, his whole paw and leg emitted a translucent light. He gasped, but drew no air. It dawned on him then that he was dead.

With his mortal eyes closed, Sahu's spirit watched Neferure pick up the ankh and run off into the night towards Apep's temple. He died before he could truly help her. Their reunion had been fleeting. Now his meagre attempt to hold on to life would be judged against him, and they would be without each other for an eternity.

He knew not what to do or where to go. For a long while he watched the stars wheel overhead, moving all too slowly. It seemed now that Sopdet would take forever to rise.

A figure emerged from the rocky Theban hillside. A tall, lanky, four-legged figure, dark and stealthy. It slunk though the desert, heading towards Sahu. Instinct told him to run from that creature, but his mind was convinced he could not. Only when the figure was close enough did the light of the stars reveal its true shape: that of the jackal god Anubis.

'I have to thank you. It makes my job much easier when a death occurs next to an entrance into Amenti.' The god's voice sounded as if spoken eons ago in a deep cavern of the underworld.

Amenti. Sahu truly was dead.

'I can't go to Amenti. I have to help Neferure.'

'You must come with me. Rise.'

Sahu looked at Anubis as if he had gone mad. 'Stand up? Does it look as if I can? I've been bitten by a cobra.'

'Rise.'

'Let's go through this again…'

'RISE.'

Anubis's voice thundered. Sahu reluctantly obeyed. He found standing easier than it had been in life. Below him lay his dead body, cold as the night. Desert wind blew across the sands and ruffled the fur upon his corpse, moving not a single hair on his translucent form.

'Now follow me.'

'Nef—'

'The affairs of the living are no longer your concern.'

'She thought me dead once. I can't inflict that pain upon her again.'

'You already have.'

Sahu stood still.

Anubis's voice bore more reason than compassion. 'Nothing more can be done here. Wandering the desert was not her hope for your eternal life. If you wish to help Neferure, you must become a transfigured spirit. Only then can you return to this earth with the power to influence the lives of mortals. You *need* to come with me.'

'If I don't pass the weighing of the heart, then what?'

Anubis smirked and turned towards the hills.

Sahu paused. What Anubis said was true; he could not help Neferure without first becoming a transfigured spirit. To do so he needed to pass the weighing of the heart ceremony. What mattered most was that Neferure stop Apep from rising upon the earth and learning the secret name of Amun-Ra. If she did not succeed, then there would be no afterworld for him to enter. He would have to take his chances with the weighing ceremony. Reluctantly Sahu followed the tracks of the jackal god.

Before long, the two of them came to a cleft in the hillside. Anubis uttered words in a language Sahu had never heard. The language of the gods sounded mysterious and older even than the lands of Egypt. Under Anubis's command, a part of the rock face vanished, revealing a tunnel leading down into the earth. Winds of great force rushed into the darkness, blowing apart Sahu's fur yet having no effect on the sand beneath his paws.

Sahu looked towards the east, across the barren sand

and beyond a thin strip of irrigated farmland. He thought he could see the shape of a boat, its white square sail illuminated by the moonlight. Was Neferure on board? He wished so.

'Come,' Anubis said, 'it is your time to be tested. You may journey back to this mortal realm after you are judged ... if you pass.'

Sahu tore his eyes from the boat, then left the star-filled sky behind as he followed Anubis into the pitch-black tunnel. They walked upon the howling wind as lightly as if they were carried upon the wings of a falcon, flown through the passageway of dark stone.

In time, the tunnel opened into a wide cavern wherein flowed a turbulent river. The waves rose sharply and forcefully as if thousands of spirits were thrashing beneath the water. Otherworldly noises echoed throughout the cavern, and an eerie blue light undulated upon the walls, emanating from below the water.

Anubis walked forward as if nothing were unusual. He leapt onto a small wooden boat shaped like an elongated crescent moon. No rope held it to the dock.

Sahu did not leave the tunnel.

'I was told that I'd have my heart weighed against a feather of Ma'at,' he said. 'However, I wasn't told anything about a river that is riddled with water dwelling demons.'

Anubis shook his head and muttered under his breath, 'Felines, never prepared.' He continued in a more audible voice. 'Have you not read and memorized the spells from the Book of the Dead?'

'No,' Sahu replied, 'I'm illiterate.'

'Very well, I will take you on a shortcut—the same one I seem to take all cats on.'

Sahu took one stiff and cautious leap onto the boat. He was unnerved at how close he stood to the river's turbulent surface. 'Why does this have to involve water?'

Anubis muttered a few derogatory remarks about felines. He voiced a spell and then clamped his jaw down upon the rudder pole. The boat glided upon the water. Howling winds chased behind them, pushing at the stern and adding to the boat's speed.

The way was sure to be long, so Sahu attempted to converse with the god before him. 'Is it not Osiris who holds judgement?' he asked.

Anubis took his mouth off the rudder pole once he had steered the boat into the middle of the river. 'For the humans, yes. Humans must pass many tests in Amenti. Of all species, they have the most trouble abiding by the laws of the gods. I used to be solely in charge of their fate, before Osiris and his council of forty-two judges took over. I have since become the god of embalming rituals and of guarding tombs ... although Meretseger handles that well enough.

'To give Osiris a much needed respite, I hold judgement for non-humans. I'm glad to keep working with Ammit.' Anubis smirked widely.

Ammit: the devourer. Sahu had heard of her before. She ate the hearts of the guilty, sending their spirits into the darkness of non-existence. He dared not imagine such a fate, the fate Neferure so greatly feared would become his.

A sudden jolt shook the boat to one side. Sahu dug his claws deep into the wooden deck. His illuminated fur puffed out at all angles. He barely heard Anubis recite a spell to calm the waters.

The rest of the journey was filled with cold silence. In time the boat came before a great golden gate guarded by two majestic, winged cobras. The boat slowed as they neared the rearing serpents. Anubis steered towards the riverbank.

'Don't I have to pass beyond those gates?' Sahu inquired.

'Did I not say I would take you on a short cut?'

The boat jerked to a halt at the edge of a new tunnel. Anubis stepped off at once and headed into the darkness. Sahu eagerly leapt onto the solid stone and followed close behind.

'Cats should really be made to learn the needed spells. Dogs always seem to find a way, perhaps because they want to earn approval from the gods,' Anubis muttered. 'Felines figure divine approval is their *right*. Always they pester someone else to do their work, whether it be learning spells or opening doors to houses.'

Sahu dropped pace, distancing himself from the jackal god. Anubis did not seem to have a great fondness for his species.

The new tunnel went on longer than the first. Sharp shapes of black rock were shrouded in darkness heavy with the scent of fear. A faint green light in the distance out-lined Anubis's form. Sahu kept his eyes upon that light, determined to face his judgement with courage.

As the last stretch through the underworld before one's final trial, the narrow tunnel bade its travellers to dwell on their coming fate. Sahu wished he knew the whereabouts of

Neferure and if she had reached the East Bank. If Ammit did not take his heart, he would go straight to Osiris and plead to return to the earth to help Neferure, if only in spirit.

When at last they reached their destination, Sahu found himself in a large cavern lit by a green mist. The mist floated in the air as a thick veil cast upon the sea. To his left was a grand scale made entirely of gold and silver. Glimmering faintly in the green light, it was set upon a stone base delicately inscribed with hieroglyphs. Resting upon one of the balances was a single pure white ostrich feather. The other balance was empty.

Teeth glinted in Sahu's mind as fiery eyes glared into his soul. He was watched by Ammit, the demon with the head of a crocodile, the front half of a lioness, and the hindquarters of a hippopotamus. She hungered always for the poisons of a heavy heart. Off to the side was where she stood waiting though the ages, hoping for the scales to tip in her favour. She alone had ended the existence of many who sought to live an eternal life. Escape was impossible once deemed guilty. Her presence made Sahu's heart pound.

Anubis moved towards the scale. He sat down, assuming a regal pose. 'I already have the feather of Ma'at, goddess of order, truth, and justice.' He looked at Sahu and continued in an offhand tone. 'All I need now is your heart.'

'My heart?' Sahu questioned. 'You will actually weigh my heart?'

'Of course,' Anubis said matter-of-factly. 'Don't worry, I shall put it back if you pass. If you do not … then it really does not matter, does it?'

Anubis gave a command in his mysterious language. Patiently he waited as Sahu's heart, the seat of all his deeds, memories, and wisdom, materialized on the balance. Ammit, ever ready to spring forth, never took her eyes off it. With exacting precision Anubis calibrated the scales, then sat back and spoke.

'Now we will find if you are to be declared true of voice. Let the judgement begin.'

Sahu waited, breathless, for the scales to tip to his demise.

CHAPTER 19

Opener of the Way

THE BALANCES WOBBLED. Ammit leaned forward, body quivering with excitement, her mouth salivating. Sahu tensed, his eyes transfixed on the scale. He might never see Neferure again. A second stretched into an eternity. The balances stopped. They had reached equilibrium. Sahu took a deep breath and relaxed his muscles.

A hieroglyph at the far end of the scale lit up with a brilliant white light. Anubis walked forward, the green mist swirling in his wake. Sahu eyed the jackal god intently, chiseling away his stone set expression, searching to reveal emotions beneath. For a long while, Anubis stared at the glyph that was alight, interpreting some meaning which seemed to be beyond his understanding. Sahu grew impatient.

'That signifies my doom ... does it not?'

Slowly Anubis turned to face him. 'The scales tell all about one's fate and the glyphs tell me the rest I need to know. I sometimes see the middle glyph illuminated. It tells me when someone arrives before their time. At that point they cannot be judged.'

Sahu waited for Anubis to continue. Soon it was clear

he did not intend to. 'What of the one that is glowing?' Sahu asked.

'That one I very rarely see alight. It tells me when those arrive who are past their time.'

It seemed to Sahu as though Anubis was purposefully vague in his answers. 'How can someone live past their time?'

A slight smirk grew upon Anubis's long and thin face. 'The reason is always different. Now we shall discover yours.'

Anubis voiced a question to the air, speaking in the dialect of the gods. Within seconds a chorus of voices responded, seemingly from the walls themselves. The council of forty-two judges conversed in their mysterious tongue. Phantom echoes of their words bounced off the stone walls and glided through Sahu's glowing form.

'It seems your full heart is not here,' Anubis said. 'Not for judgement anyway.'

Fear and tension boiled to anger. Sahu flattened his ears and whiskers. 'Do the gods of the underworld always speak in riddles, or is it just a habit of yours?'

Anubis brushed the subject aside and continued. 'The riddle of your life, as revealed to me by Amun-Ra, is an interesting one. It appears that you have sacrificed your heart to aid another cat, with full knowledge of your own inevitable fate.'

Sahu's ears perked forward. 'That's what this is about, me escaping death to help Neferure?'

'It would appear so.'

'You said my full heart was not there for judgement. Where is the rest?'

'She has the rest.'

'You mean that literally?'

'Of course not. How would that be possible? I mean it in the metaphysical sense.'

'Why can't you calibrate the scale to compensate?'

Anubis voiced a growl sounding vaguely like a human's laugh. 'If things were that simple, Ammit here would have my job. The scale cannot be calibrated to compensate because part of someone still living resides upon it. This is an exchange I have only seen twice before.'

'No. This can't be.' Sahu realized what had happened. 'Neferure promised she would do anything to keep me from being judged guilty, but I can't let her do this. Please, Anubis, return things to the way they should be, and I will accept my judgement as it is.'

'This cannot be undone. Your judgement will not take place at this time.' Anubis looked towards the base of the scale. 'You see how the glyph on the end has stopped glowing and the one near the top has become illuminated?'

'Yes.'

'It means your time has been extended. Not only that, but Amun-Ra has gifted you with something rather unique: nine lives. However, due to your recklessness today and your escape from death by fire before, you have only seven remaining. I shall wait for you to assimilate this information. Many times Osiris has reprimanded me for overburdening the minds of mortals.'

Anubis waited patiently. He had far greater reserve than most canines, Sahu noted.

Sahu processed the information quicker than the jackal god seemed to expect. 'Why was I gifted this? Have I not offended the gods by betraying a servant of theirs?'

'Amun-Ra would not reveal his reasons to me. He only told me the rules. I would guess that since we cannot interfere directly in the physical world, and since Apep has clouded our view of the mortal realm, our hopes for winning this war with him lie with you and Neferure.

Anubis paced around Sahu, his lithe form gliding through the illuminated mist. 'You will live until you lose the remainder of your lives, and we will not be able to complete the weighing of either of your hearts until you both die. Is this clear?'

'Yes. Unexpected, but very clear.'

Sahu wondered about his good fortune. Only minutes before he faced the possibility of being denied an eternal life. Now he was being sent back with the ability to walk through death itself. How was he supposed to find his way out through the tunnels of the underworld? He'd need more than nine lives to accomplish that without Anubis's guidance.

A great roar filled the cavern, rumbling in the ground and rushing through the tunnels in a wave of echoes.

'Apep is readying himself to challenge Ra.' Anubis shook his head. 'Apep has lost every battle as steady as the sun rises, but the war he prepares for may yet bring chaos to all.'

Another jackal entered the hall. He came through a passageway Sahu was sure did not exist moments before. Unlike Anubis he was not black as night, but rather a brownish grey. He stood proudly on the spot where he had entered. Anubis spoke next.

'This is Upuaut: The Opener of the Way. He will guide you back through the caverns of the underworld to your body and then beyond the desert you seek to pass. Have you any more questions?'

'How will I know when I've lost another life?'

'You will know. Death shall pass through you.'

Sahu prepared himself to leave, walking towards Upuaut. He turned and looked back.

'Just one more thing,' Sahu said. Anubis fixed an iron stare upon him. 'I would like to have my heart back.'

One last smirk grew upon Anubis's shadowy face. The hall and all its gods washed away before Sahu's eyes.

A breeze came and rushed over Sahu's fur as the tips of many feathers. Breath entered his body. He opened his mortal eyes to see Upuaut gazing down upon him.

'Isis has given you life,' the god declared. 'May her wings protect you in the upcoming battle.'

Ahmes stood before Heqaib beneath the stars upon his roof. The air was unusually chilly. Wind ruffled their fur and picked up the edges of a thin papyrus scroll. Only the weight of Heqaib's paw kept the scroll from escaping into the night. Hissing and yowling spread through the dark streets as the plague voiced its victory over Thebes. Attacks from both strays and housecats came unexpectedly and viciously to those who had not sought safety.

'Do you know what this is?' Heqaib looked down at the unrolled document. Strength had drained from his body, and his front paws shook beneath his weight. Unlike most cats, the plague did not cause anger to boil in Heqaib. He had always been different.

'Some kind of papyrus scroll.' Ahmes had no clue what Heqaib expected her to say.

'Yes.' Heqaib wheezed as he drew air. 'This is a very special scroll. Within it lies all the known ways to defeat Apep: magical rites, utterances, and spells. I must ask something very important of you. I would do this myself if I were not so ill.'

For a moment, Ahmes hesitated. 'What is it?' she asked with a hint of anger. Her tail twitched.

'I need you to memorize and deliver one of these spells to the old cat who sleeps in the hypostyle hall of Karnak Temple. He'll know what to do with it.'

Ahmes pressed her ears back. 'What do you mean? That old cat never even moves. Why him?'

'I fear there's little time to explain.' Heqaib set his eyes towards the east. 'Dark clouds are closing in. Neferure must have known something important; she never bothered bringing me anything to translate before. Trust me when I say this must be done immediately and that Khu will understand.'

'The old cat's name is Khu? How do you know that?' Ahmes asked.

Heqaib drew a long wheezy breath of air as he travelled far back into his memory. 'I knew Khu during my youth, when I travelled to Abydos. He often came to me for knowledge. Both of us were followers of Thoth. We grew apart when it became clear to him I could not provide the sort of knowledge he sought.'

Ahmes considered Heqaib's request. A curt nod indicated her agreement. It took Heqaib only two repetitions of the spell before Ahmes had memorized it to the word

'Normally this spell would be accompanied by casting wax figures and papyrus images of Apep into the fires of burning khesau grass,' Heqaib said. 'For now the words themselves must do.'

'Dangerous words, dangerous rituals. These probably should never see the light of day,' Ahmes said.

'Don't worry about that. Please, go now and hurry.'

Neferure set a trembling paw upon solid ground. She shook water from her drenched fur, biting down hard upon the ankh. Behind her the old man shouted profanities for having driven his boat too far into the marshlands.

Waves of shivers slithered around Neferure's body, both from the cold of the water and from the plague. If only there'd been an actual dock for her to land upon she would not be so soaked. *Humans are always inefficient*, she thought angrily, flattening her ears in disgust and scampering off into the tall grasses of the farmland.

She did not care if she ran into any strays. They had no right to dictate her path or alter her course.

Sand and grit stuck to Neferure's wet fur and embedded in her skin. She was dirty, wet, and cold—and hated all of it.

Neferure made it to the desert without any confrontations. She was certain the strays could sense the fire burning in her claws. They did not dare challenge her again.

The eastern Theban hills rose in the distance as a wall of shadows from the earth, concealing Apep's temple behind their guard.

Neferure looked down as she ran. Even the light of the moon now stung her eyes. Along the way her left leg wobbled. In mid-stride her muscles gave out, and her weak body tumbled into the sands. Shaking, she picked herself up and ambled towards the dim horizon.

Time passed as she struggled slowly across the desert. Many new stars sprung up and sailed past the skyline. Dark clouds strengthened in the east. Eventually, after much painful travel, Neferure found herself trembling under the tall shadows of the eastern hillside.

Her muscles were crumbling and turning to water. Paw by paw she gripped rock, making a weak attempt to crawl up the jagged hillside. With half-closed eyes, she sought out each new foothold.

All of her pain was Sahu's fault! He should have seen signs of the plague growing in her. He died and took the easy way out because he did not want to help defeat Apep. Even the gods had abandoned her. Where was Bast? Where was the great goddess of cats? The gods were rejoicing while she was dying.

They're all cowards! Neferure yelled as her diseased mind lost its grip on reality.

Her claws retracted, and she lost her footing. Wildly scraping the air, her paws sought for solid ground as she fell. She hit a round rock and rolled over it, tumbling roughly down the steep hillside. Her small body struck rock after rock, and the ankh fell from her mouth.

When the hills were done with her, she was tossed

roughly onto the ground. Her body pulsed in pain. There she lay, weak, battered, and unable to stand.

Moments later, the ankh impacted the sands.

───ᴥ∿ᴕ───

The ambush the housecats set up was effective. The line of strays broke, and they scampered away with their tails between their legs. Khakhati was left with all manner of scratches from the battle, but the victory pleased him.

Khakhati looked to the two cats closest to him. 'Send word to Ahmes to amass as many housecats as possible.' He strode to another rooftop. 'Have all housecats scour the city for Qetu. We must find him.'

His orders delivered, Khakhati looked up at the darkened sky. Clouds from the east were beginning to veil the stars. If Ahmes was indeed the cat working with Apep, there would be no reinforcements.

Khakhati moved steadily toward the city, searching for The Word or Qetu, although he had no clue where to start. 'Maahes, grant me a sign so that we can defeat this evil,' he muttered.

An awful crushing noise swept around Khakhati's ears. He crouched low and listened. A thin woman stepped heavily upon the tall grasses and soft ground. Her expensive sandals were stained with mud. Minutes later a wisp of fine white linen floated before his eyes. Looking up, he saw that it was Kesi. Soundlessly and attentively Khakhati followed the woman as she ploughed her way through the grasses. Soon she met up with a middle-aged man who was standing still and looking forlorn. He recognized the man as the vizier of Lower Egypt. Khakhati dug his claws into the soil. These people were, without doubt, the Followers.

Khakhati raised his nose to the black sky and sniffed at the cool air, picking up much sweat and fear. Something was amiss.

Qetu paced. His hands fidgeted with the pleats on his fine linen kilt. 'Our leader was supposed to be here already.'

'He will harm us for not having found it.' Kesi threw up her arms. 'All our efforts have been in vain ... where are the others?'

'They were told to stay away—unless any of them found The Word.'

Kesi narrowed her eyes. 'Clearly that has not happened.'

Khakhati's claws pierced further into the soil, his spine stiffened into an arch. Having seen the Followers with his own eyes, the reality and consequences of their plot struck him. More than just a battle to fight, the fate of Egypt was at stake.

A delicate hand reached through the grasses and parted the curtain of green. A pedicured foot gracefully stepped out upon the mud. The woman who floated forward bore royal jewellery, her face impassive and symmetrical as a stone effigy to Isis: Queen Tiye. Two paces behind her were four of her elite soldiers with their hands on the hilt of their swords. They were the ruthless assassins that Queen Tiye used to dispatch her enemies. The queen turned towards the vizier. 'I know what you are up to.'

Qetu gasped. Sweat beaded upon his brow. His eyes darted as he looked for an escape route. A heavy hand met his shoulder and held him still. Qetu swivelled around, coming face-to-face with Khesef-hra. Relief flooded his face as he saw his leader.

Khesef-hra was not smiling.

Relief ebbed into disdain.'You wretch, you were followed!' he shouted at Kesi. The air crackled with tension as Qetu counted the odds. Even if they managed to escape, Queen Tiye would reveal them to Ramesses.

As beads of sweat dripped into Qetu's eye, Khesef-hra took two steps forward. He moved quickly to Tiye's side. Laughing, he slid his hand up her back, drawing away her hair, and planted a kiss to her neck. 'We mustn't tease Qetu. The man has been very helpful to our cause and does not deserve to die of fright.'

Tiye responded with a one-sided smile.

Kesi bowed to her queen, then turned to Qetu. 'Queen Tiye is our true leader. She revived our cult while I served as her eyes and ears within the Followers. You must understand, with her position, why she couldn't reveal herself sooner.'

Stunned, Qetu stood rooted to the ground.

'Won't you bow before your Queen and leader?' Khesef-hra asked.

Qetu nodded, then bowed deeply. 'If I may ask: why? What do you have to gain? I will soon be vizier of Upper and Lower Egypt, but you?'

Tiye jutted her chin. 'Ramesses has betrayed me, and he's betrayed Egypt. He was mistaken not to name Pentawer his successor.' Water gathered in Tiye's eyes. 'My son shall be pharaoh, not some foreigner's son. He will lead our country away from bankruptcy and restore the glory that once was.

Looking to Khesef-hra, she cleared her throat. 'And I will have the man I always wanted.' She moved to put her arms upon the high priest, but her movements seemed calculated and insincere to Khakhati's eyes. Khesef-hra inflated his chest upon her touch.

'These are but dreams now. We've failed to figure out the riddle,' Qetu stammered, avoiding the high priest's thundering gaze. 'The words tell us nothing.'

> *It is hidden in whence it all began,*
> *Over which the Nile long has ran.*
> *Still waters have forever kept it clean,*
> *Resting upon ground long unseen.'*

Khesef-hra interrupted.

> *'Year upon year has always passed,*
> *Celebrations to which solar light was cast.'*

'I have solved the riddle,' he continued in his deep, baritone voice. 'It speaks of the Opet festival, when Amun-Ra's solar barque sails across the sacred lake of Karnak Temple—the lake through which the Nile flows, which has never been emptied. It was there, at the bottom of the lake, tangled in the oldest of lotus roots.'

The high priest then held up an amulet: the Tyet knot made of the blood of Isis. Its garnet stone glowed softly with a divine inner light, a full moon shining among a carnelian sunset.

'I have found The Word.'

CHAPTER 20

The Word

NO CAT OF Per-Maahes has fully lived up to Ibenre's name, but likewise none has disgraced their title, Khakhati thought, replaying his own words in his head. The Word is out of my reach. However, if I amass the nearby strays, then even if Ahmes does not bring reinforcements, I may be able to change the tide of the battle.

Mehen's moon-cast shadow loomed over Khakhati's tensed face. The two cats stood within view of the city. Tall emmer wheat grasses stuck out from the rich soil, concealing them from view.

'I heard of the recent schism among the strays.' Khakhati stood rooted to the ground and drew his shoulders back. 'This is a time of evil. Our species, whether stray or house-cat, may suffer along with all life in Egypt.'

Mehen flattened his ears, arched his spine and let out a low growl. 'Didn't you find your job surprisingly easy when I was still their leader?'

Khakhati recoiled his head. 'Because no strays tried to re-enter the city until now does not mean my job was easy.

I had to keep sentinels posted, keep track of what they'd seen—'

'Your job was easy and uneventful because I influenced the strays.' Mehen began circling Khakhati. 'Trying to convince sick and angry strays that housecats have nothing to do with the plague is much more difficult than asking cats to stare at the horizon. I was succeeding—until full power was taken from me.'

Khakhati traced Mehen's path with his eyes. 'What good will come of convincing me you should have been initiated into Per-Maahes instead of my mother? I can tell you why you don't have her amulet around your neck. It's because respect is beyond your understanding.'

Mehen twitched his tail and turned to leave. 'I would not protect that which I don't respect.'

'Then help me guard the two cats whose mission matters most,' Khakhati said, 'even though one of them is a betrayer of Ma'at.'

Mehen paused. 'Explain, and I shall decide.'

'Very well.' Khakhati stared directly into Mehen's eyes. 'Just remember that our actions will forever be recorded in our hearts.'

'The path to Apep's temple is near.' Upuaut led Sahu, in his mortal form, through a grey and foggy tunnel of the underworld.

Dark shapes of spirits rushed across their path. Upuaut fended off each apparition with a unique spell. Sahu watched everything with eyes only half-aware; he was still deeply shaken by his encounter with death. He had much to accomplish and little time to dwell upon his narrowly avoided fate.

'How am I to cross the Nile?' Sahu asked, looking as far ahead through the fog as possible.

'The Nile is already long behind us,' Upuaut replied. 'The paths of the underworld are unaffected by earthly terrain, yet distance must still be trod.'

Many paces later the tunnel drew to its end. The heavy fog dissipated, revealing a night sky dusted with shimmering white stars. Sahu rushed out and found himself standing below a tall peak in the rocky hillside east of Thebes—the same rise concealing Apep's hideous temple. Looking behind, he could see Upuaut waiting inside the tunnel. Mist swirled around the lithe jackal god but never went past the gateway to the underworld.

'I cannot take you any further,' Upuaut said, a hint of fear in his voice. His long ears were drawn back. 'It is an evil place into which you venture. Beware of your surroundings, even what is made of stone.'

Taking Upuaut's warning to heart, Sahu then turned to face the dark hillside. His pupils dilated to compensate for the lack of light. Ominous thunderclouds were building in the east and spreading across the sky like a swarm of locusts. A familiar scent blew towards him, and his sharp eyes narrowed upon a golden cat lying at the base of the hillside. 'Neferure!'

Sahu tore through the cold sands towards where she lay, stopping to nuzzle her limp body.

Neck muscles trembled as Neferure summoned the

strength to lift her head off the ground, wearily gazing at Sahu through half-closed eyelids.

'Apep is clouding the heavens so the light of Sopdet cannot pierce his eyes.' She looked past rather than at him and drew one deep rattling breath.

'Light of Sopdet?'

'Thoth said the answer lies in the light of Isis's star. I possess the power to stop Apep. Not that there's use now in trying. The Followers have arrived at the temple. I saw them walking in the distance. I heard them talk about The Word. They've found it. Everything's over and it's all your fault.'

A surge of anger pulsed in Sahu's nerves. *His fault?* How could that be? He'd done everything in his power to help. He averted his glance to the sand, passing his gaze over Neferure's raw bite wound. Sahu paused. A jolt of clear understanding charged through him. 'Neferure, that's not you talking. It's Apep's plague.'

No response came. The air grew frigid and the land turned silent.

'Your promise,' Sahu said. 'Your promise saved me from death. I said I would always be there for you, but I can't help you if you don't let me.'

Neferure slowly looked into Sahu's eyes. 'Is this another one of your lies? Another promise you plan to break?'

In one long heartbeat her eyes closed, and Neferure's head of golden fur fell as a rock onto the sands.

Ahmes turned to her right and walked through the plethora of stone columns to reach the end of the hypostyle hall. Khu was there, predictably fast asleep against the south wall, under a carved and painted depiction of Ramesses II binding together the two lands of Upper and Lower Egypt. Ahmes batted Khu a few times with her paw, seeing if she could wake him. Nothing. Khu did not even twitch.

Setting aside her hesitation, Ahmes delivered the spell in its entirety to the sleeping lump before her. Then she stood still, waiting to see what affect her words had. Only the steady rise and fall of Khu's chest told her he was still alive.

'I forgot to mention this is the spell to defeat Apep,' she said to break the silence. 'Heqaib told me to give it to you.'

Ahmes waited moments longer, still hoping for any reaction.

'Well, I'll be going now.'

As if he knew I was there at all, she thought to herself. Perhaps Heqaib was starting to go senile. Ahmes walked off, a growl bidding to exit her throat. Hunting was a more useful pastime anyway.

Through the shady hall moved the silhouette of a cat carrying a serpentine figure. The silhouette paused and changed direction, heading towards Ahmes. Dull moonlight washed out the small amount of colour in the cat's fur. Around the cat's neck was a folded sheet of papyrus strung upon a collar made of rough rope, looking like an amulet. Vexation was written into every subtle facial expression.

Ahmes perked her ears forward and fanned out her whiskers. 'Aren't you Neferure's sister?' she asked.

Takhaet froze. She dropped the figure to the ground. It appeared to be made of wax. 'I don't claim relation to cats who associate with strays. Was that you I heard reciting a spell?'

'What spell?'

Takhaet laughed. 'The spell to stop Apep, of course. If your last weapon is that ... thing,' she glanced at Khu, 'then you may as well work on your grovelling towards the great god of chaos. Only that will save you.'

Ahmes titled her head. 'What is going on? You aren't making any sense.'

'I am the only one who makes sense,' declared Takhaet.

'And what is that around your neck?'

'A message.' Vexation deepened upon Takhaet's face. 'Along with rope not fine enough for my fur.'

Hunting for mice was easier than hunting for information. Interrogation was not Ahmes's forte, and she was grateful that Takhaet gloated so readily. 'Why are you holding an ankh then?'

'I will tell you, for nothing now can save you.' Takhaet's haughty voice carried no trace of regret. 'I've allied myself with the Followers of Apep. These ankhs will allow manifestations of our god to rise. They're inscribed with the necessary spells.'

At first Ahmes had thought Neferure's paranoia was invented. Now, knowing more of the truth, knowing that Takhaet was the traitor Neferure had spoken of, her anger towards her friend grew into deep concern. What had happened to her in the meantime?

'The Followers have found the secret name of Amun-Ra,'

Takhaet boasted. 'Now there is no stopping Apep's rising.' She looked at Ahmes in mockery. 'I suppose it doesn't hurt to mention I placed one wax figure of Apep in a very convenient location—a location that will allow for a quick and effortless change in the power structure of this land.'

Ahmes tilted her head, seconds passing before she figured out the clue. Her hackles raised in fright. Unknowingly she unsheathed her claws. 'You mean a manifestation of Apep will come to power in Egypt by killing the pharaoh?'

'Excellent work.' Takhaet started grooming her left shoulder. 'Although, Apep himself would never be bothered ruling these lands. One of The Followers is close in line for the throne. They each earn their distinct rewards.'

'What might yours be?' Ahmes asked.

'Soon I will be worshipped in place of Bast. Then, of course, will be the complete elimination of strays.' Takhaet turned her head sharply away. In doing so, the fur on her left shoulder parted and revealed a small scar, violent looking and deep, as only a stray would cause. Unaware of this she turned back to Ahmes. 'Now, shouldn't you be off doing what you do best? Killing serpents and defending the pharaoh?'

Ahmes snapped to her senses. 'If anything happens to Ramesses, I will hunt you down and kill you.' Twitching her tail, she ran back through the forest of stone columns. She would do what she was born for. This was a true test of her lineage. She would die before she let any harm come to Ramesses.

Neferure felt her head slam onto the ground, her ear gathering fine sand granules within its cusp. She observed, rather than experienced, all sensations, as if she and her body were now two separate beings. Not once did her eyes close. The stinging pain from the lunar light was no longer connected to her vision. All that tied her to her body was a raging fire of anger, burning and consuming her, dancing along with the moving shapes she saw appear on the horizon.

From Thebes it came. A living cloud formed, silhouettes skimming the desert earth. Was it coming for her? Perhaps the chaos of Apep was sweeping throughout Egypt and consuming all that was of Ma'at? Indeed, Neferure had failed. Sahu had failed her.

She became faintly aware *he* was still speaking to her—from beyond the grave. Sahu had taken a coward's way out of danger and now was trying to offer help from a place of safety. He had practically walked into death ... and now wanted her quick and effortless forgiveness.

'Neferure, the strays are coming. Can you not see them?' Sahu's voice resonated through her blanket of anger.

Tightening her blurry vision Neferure observed, from afar, silhouettes take the form of many cats.

Sahu continued to speak, his words blending together as they echoed through her brain. 'I can't tell if the strays are being led by Mehen or those cats who turned against him. Likely they are coming to kill us.'

I don't care, Neferure thought. *The strays are all betrayers. Mehen has betrayed us just as you have betrayed me.* She was taken by a strong urge to lash out with her claws and strike Sahu in the face.

Softening his eyes, Sahu stood stoic. 'I know that words, however well phrased, can do little to cool your anger.' He inhaled one deep breath. 'Know that I came back from death to protect you, to help.'

Came back from death? A new and unrecognized feeling, lying far beyond pain or anger, filtered into Neferure's blood and gave her new strength. She struggled to her paws, muscles aching, burning with the plague's wrath, not wanting her to see the quest through to its completion.

'Prove it,' she said. Neferure looked Sahu in the eye and unsheathed her claws.

Without waiting for an answer, Neferure staggered towards where the ankh lay. Balanced uneasily on all four paws, she bent her neck to grab Akhotep's sacred jewellery. She swayed, and Sahu was there to brace her. Her jaws quivered under her orders to grasp the heavy metal. The ankh's solid weight dragged her head towards the ground, and struggling against it helped to force awareness to her muscles and stabilize her now feeble body.

With Sahu aiding her every step, Neferure attempted once more to ascend the steep Theban hills.

In many areas the rocks were loose and fragile, making for unsure footing. Neferure tested each step before placing weight upon her paws. She knew she was dying. The next time she fell would be her last, and then her nightmare of Egypt's ruin would come to pass. Fear propelled her aching joints forward even as her muscles quivered. Each time she slipped Sahu was there to hold her steady. Under his guidance they passed the midway point on the hill, not once looking down. Their path was long, the hilltop reaching to touch the surface of the liquid black sky.

A rumbling began beneath their paws. Vibrations grew in power as they emerged, racing towards the heavens. A hollow and angry roar broke loose. Trees snapped and stones were hurled violently into the air, hitting the trembling ground as gravity claimed hold. The Nile split into many waves that fought back at the land, their torment working to quell the earth's rage.

'I heard this in the underworld.' Sahu turned to Neferure as they clung desperately to the hillside. 'It is the voice of Apep.'

When the grounds quieted Neferure and Sahu resumed their slow struggle, digging their claws deep into rock both solid and crumbling. Dust rose in their faces, clogging their noses. Together they clambered up towards the night sky and its growing veil of storm clouds.

Paw by paw they gradually reached the hill's summit. With the barrier of rock now beneath them, a clear panoramic sight of the land below unfolded.

Khesef-hra stood inside the inner sanctum of Apep's fragmented temple, facing the altar. His robes billowed in the wind. With one steady and calculated gesture, the high priest placed the Tyet knot of Isis onto the cold black stone, before the sight of the gold-cast serpent.

'How will Apep keep the Followers from hearing The Word?' Sahu wondered aloud.

'Just as The Word was transferred from Ra's heart into Isis's,' Neferure spoke in a barely suppressed hiss, 'so it shall pass from the amulet into the black heart of Apep.'

From the ground Khesef-hra lifted a ceramic jug filled

with water and methodically poured it over the amulet, letting the excess spill over the stone and soak into the hungry ground. The scent of steeped lotus blossoms spread throughout the air.

As the water evaporated, the amulet spoke the words of the conversation last held: a contention between mighty gods.

Ra's dying cries pounded through the desert, howling across the vast cold sands. The voice of Isis soared as fluidly around Ra's words as a hawk amidst a storm, hunting for his secret name.

Sahu looked over at Neferure. She clutched an ankh tightly in her trembling jaws and unsteadily hurried down the steep and uneven rocks.

CHAPTER 21

Apep

INSIDE THE PALACE walls, life was silent. The administrative building Ahmes entered was devoid of a single breathing creature besides herself. Decisions affecting all of Egypt were made daily in this room. The decor was of high elegance and sophistication, viewed only by the elite. A golden throne, inlaid with the most prized of jewels, was placed in the centre of the room. On top of an ornate table was a scale model and architectural plans for the building of Ramesses's own addition to the temple complex at Karnak.

Rooted to the spot, Ahmes shifted her focus to her paws and felt for vibrations of subtle movement upon the stone-tiled floor. Nothing. She attentively scanned all empty spaces in the room with her eyes, her ears kept open and her whiskers fanned outward, rotating and testing for minute changes in the air currents. Again, nothing. Ahmes broke from complete stillness into a quick and graceful run. She passed a pair of armed guards on her route towards the pharaoh's private quarters.

A short path through an immaculately manicured garden led Ahmes's way. She knew every inch of the palace, as well as the scents, mannerisms, and habits of those who dwelt within it. She knew where she would most likely find the pharaoh. Ahmes entered through a doorway, then tore through a spacious, columned hall that gave way to a small antechamber.

The silhouette of a stately man stood before a large, easterly window. Deep in meditative thought, his face was impassive. Rarely were Egyptian skies cloudy, and his eyes sought to pierce through the chaos forming on the horizon; he was searching for the evils blocking the rising light of Sopdet.

Just as Ra was ignorant of the snake Isis had set before his path, Ramesses was now so focused upon the tempest overtaking the skies that he did not notice certain death slithering behind him.

Ahmes sounded a frantic yowl.

~ ⚜ ~

'Be wary of your surroundings,' Sahu warned as he remembered Upuaut's words, 'even what is made of stone.'

Neferure gave no indication that she'd heard his warning. He held his breath as he watched her rush down the treacherous rocks. She did not so much run as fall forward down the hillside, continually bracing herself upright with trembling legs. Clouds of dust rose from under her paws and suffocated her path.

She hit the flat sands the moment the wave of strays reached the hill's peak. A spray of dirt and rocks crashed down in their wake. Spine arched, tail thrashing, claws unsheathed, Sahu turned to block their way.

A glint of red light reflected towards the heavens. Khakhati ran with a small group of housecats, taken from their stations upon the rooftops. Mehen and the strays charged alongside. Sahu stood down.

'Sahu!' Khakhati yowled as he stormed past. 'Ahmes is a traitor. She never came with reinforcements. She should be killed upon our return.'

Neferure's words resounded, racing through Sahu's mind: *One of The Followers can hear us speak.* 'The hand-maiden,' Sahu warned Khakhati. 'Careful. She can hear what you say.'

The vizier fearfully glanced sideways at the pack of strays roaring down the rocks. With flailing hands he searched the ground for as many stones as he could reach, grasping for any kind of weapon lying by the temple. Kesi slowly and cautiously took backward steps, keeping her venomous gaze trained upon Khakhati's garnet eye of Horus. Tiye stood strong; only her hand clenching onto an inch of her white dress betrayed her fear. Her guards surrounded her.

Sahu chased after the strays, tearing down the hillside to join them in combat. He suppressed the pain of the sharp rocks as they ripped into his paw pads. A stolen glance through the temple's broken walls revealed that Neferure had almost reached Apep's altar. Her path had been slowed by the presence of Khesef-hra.

Neferure was hiding behind the stone wall that encased Apep's inner sanctum. Her muscles were shaking violently, and her grip on the Akhotep's ankh was loosening. She lay it hastily upon the sand and pressed herself tightly against the shattered stone. He needed to help her.

Khesef-hra swept his eyes across the terrain, ensuring the security of Isis's amulet. He began circling the altar, peering around fallen columns and behind walls, edging his way to where Neferure hid.

Storm clouds blocked every star in the sky. The dialogue between Isis and Ra raged like the cold winds that tore across the lands. Isis' persistence was as calculating and precise as the eyes of a lioness stalking elusive prey.

Kesi's loud shriek pierced Sahu's ears like a lance. He turned and saw several strays dashing towards the handmaiden. Qetu launched several rocks at the cats. In turn, he was met by a swarm of strays and housecats biting and clawing at his legs and feet. The vizier kicked hard at his attackers. Kesi retreated, hurling stones, hitting Qetu more often than she did a cat, and shrieking again when Khakhati and two strays broke off, heading towards her.

One small rock met its target. Khakhati yowled as the impact struck him from the side. A moment of fear took hold of his expression as he fell into the sand. Swiftly he regained his footing. Again stoic, he nonetheless sought temporary refuge from the battle, a slight limp in his gait.

'I must help Neferure,' Sahu said as Khakhati drew near. 'You distract the high priest.'

'How?

The thundering gaze of Khesef-hra crashed down upon Sahu. Khakhati flattened his ears and hissed at the high priest.

A devious glint grew in Sahu's eyes. 'Steal The Word.'

Night gave Apep's broken temple a wild and demonic presence, a gateway that led deeper and deeper into the heart of chaos. Sahu entered the temple through the winding avenue of rearing stone serpents. They looked down at him with ravenous eyes, poised to strike. Evil festered in the very stone that formed them.

The eyes of the high priest fixed upon Sahu and Akhotep's ankh. Khesef-hra did not notice Khakhati navigating his way directly though the broken walls at the southern side of the temple, towards Apep's hematite altar. With his deep baritone voice, Khesef-hra spoke a short and powerful spell.

Sandstone transformed into green scales. Carved eyes became darkened windows peering into the coldest depths of space. Fangs turned from rock into silver shards of ice. Life breathed into the stone serpent guardians of Apep's temple. Sahu froze. His heart picked up pace. Upuaut's warning had come to pass.

Along the entire avenue, the stone serpents stretched, raising their heads to the sky, wavering, then striking down onto the earth. In size they dwarfed the cobra sent by Meretseger. From the start of the avenue they advanced, following their call to protect the inner sanctum.

Sahu's fur stood on end. For a moment he wondered by what ancient magic the serpents had been awakened. Coming to his senses, he ran through the misshapen hypostyle hall and down past the broken pylons, vestibules and dilapidated chambers. The serpents followed in slow pursuit, adjusting to their new muscles.

Khesef-hra's eyes followed Sahu's every move. As Sahu neared the inner sanctum the high priest bade the serpents to hasten, and they heeded his demands. Sahu waited outside the walls of the inner sanctum for Khakhati to arrive and steal The Word. His eyes flew up to the stars. Sopdet was concealed behind storm clouds. How could Neferure channel the energy of a shrouded star?

The high priest glanced at the serpents and gave a wicked smile, baring his teeth like an old hunting dog. He gave a glance toward the ankh he had placed upright in a slot upon the altar's surface days ago. He began to chant. The sand and the stone and the heavens resonated with his rich, deep notes. For a moment Sahu's memory walked along the secluded torch-lit halls of Karnak, returning to a time when Khesef-hra sang soulful hymns for the enjoyment of Amun-Ra.

As the chanting continued, a section of storm clouds began to part. The star Thuban shone through the sky, passing its dim light through the centre of Khesef-hra's ankh, magnifying it upon the gold cast serpent.

A ghastly hollow roar struck out from the ground, overpowering the contention between Isis and Ra. As it ate up the star's light, the golden statue of Apep began to manifest a living essence. Golden scales melted to vibrant green, and the statue's garnet eyes blackened from flame to shadow. Slowly, Apep was rising upon the earth, gaining a living heart so that The Word might be transferred into it.

Sahu glanced behind. The horde of serpentine figures was slithering forward. Death was at his heels. Khesef-hra stood in front of the altar, his back to the Tyet amulet and his ears ignoring the speech of gods. Through impatient eyes he anxiously waited for the slow-moving serpents to cover more ground.

Khakhati leapt silently from the shadows and onto the glossy surface of the hematite altar, paws bracing him from sliding. He batted Khesef-hra's ankh to the ground. Apep's rising ceased. The golden serpent crystallized into a half-living entity, looking out into the night with short-sighted vision. Khakhati snatched Isis's amulet in his mouth and jumped from the altar. He met the ground soundlessly and sped off towards the housecats.

Khesef-hra's face contorted first into fear, then anger. He strode purposefully after Khakhati, exiting the temple and leaving a whirlwind of sand in his wake.

'Neferure!' Sahu ran to meet her where she stood—at the northern wall encasing the inner sanctum.

Her muscles trembled and her breaths heaved. Her claws were gripping to the soft sand. Rigid and hunched, she pressed up against the stone wall.

'Neferure!' Sahu called her name again. 'You must finish this!'

Her eyes and ears struggled to focus.

Sahu stepped closer. 'You've made it this far. Ignore the serpents. I'll protect you and fend them off. You must hurry. I fear Apep will soon receive The Word.

Breaths eased, claws retracted, yet still Neferure did not look Sahu in the eye. He eased her to her feet.

Slowly and cautiously she moved toward Akhotep's ankh. Her muscles trembled, and with each step she staggered. She grasped Akhotep's ankh in her mouth, then stumbled into the doorway of the inner sanctum. Apep's eyes shifted backwards, focusing upon her.

Sahu's ear swivelled backwards. He turned and swiped

at a serpent moments before it struck.

The snake aimed at Sahu's front legs and struck again. He leapt backwards, rearing up onto his hindquarters and slashing at the serpent as it edged forward. In one well-placed strike, he gashed the snake across its face, between its eyes and nose, thus damaging its ability to sense heat and find prey in complete darkness. The serpent sharply recoiled.

Sahu moved closer to Neferure until he was standing within the sanctum's doorway. 'Go while the high priest is distracted!'

One serpent slithered towards Neferure. Sahu jumped in front of it, slashing wildly to protect her. Neferure flattened her ears and took many slow and faltering steps towards Apep's altar.

In the midst of battle, Sahu stole a glance to the side. He couldn't see Khakhati or catch sight of his garnet amulet. Khesef-hra was heading back to the temple, Isis's Tyet amulet in his hand. Several strays swarmed the high priest, slashing at his feet and knees. Khesef-hra let out a howl of pain and ploughed towards the outer wall of the temple. One stray climbed the broken stone and launched himself at the high priest, landing on his shoulder and digging his claws into linen and skin, refusing to let go. The other strays followed his daring example.

Finally Neferure reached the base of the altar. The charred crimson eyes of Apep in his semi-risen state focused upon her. Neferure bit down upon Akhotep's ankh. She met Apep's gaze.

'Turn. Turn away from here and rid yourself of that tool.' Apep spoke out from the earth in a rich, alluring tone. 'You have allowed your mind to play tricks on you. You placed your trust in gods who do nothing to stop the sickness invading Egypt. I am blamed for their inadequacy. By destroying me, you are destroying all hope. Turn. Turn away from here and rid yourself of that tool.'

Neferure paused, her gaze transfixed upon Apep's statue.

'What are you doing?!' Sahu yowled as he fought off a growing number of living stone serpents, strays joining to help. 'Neferure! Ignore him! He has no real power over you.'

Apep's eyes deepened and his voice became increasingly seductive. 'Turn your back on Sahu. His is a mind tricked by the gods. Do not let yourself fall into the same trap. The gods speak evil through him. He is only using you to destroy me. I am the only one who will be here long after he abandons you in the name of his gods. Turn. Turn your—'

'Neferure, listen to me.' Sahu paused to fight off one vengeful serpent. 'You know in your heart that Apep's words are lies. I will always stand by your side as I'm doing right now. Shut your ears to his poison. Just ki—'

A pair of sharp silver fangs pierced Sahu's shoulder, exchanging blood for poison. Death took time passing through him. Soft feathers of Isis's divine wings embraced him, suspending him in a heavenly cloud of complete peace. He could see nothing but pure light. He was part of a song in the breath of the divine and he could have lived forever as a single note. Nothing else mattered, and no other world existed. Suddenly the heavenly cloud shattered as he was brought back to life. Agony rained through Sahu's body. His wound pounded as if his bones were being smashed against rock.

Sahu's eyes refocused on the world before him. The serpents were constricting around him, tightening the atmosphere. Several were headed to protect the hematite altar. A wall now separated Khesef-hra from the inner sanctum. Neferure still stood transfixed by Apep's stare. Her mind, clouded from the plague's effects, was unable to see through his lies. The god of chaos listened, unhindered, to the divine conversation streaming through the air, a subtly wicked smile carved upon his face.

Ramesses spun and glared at the snake. He called for his guards and for his weapons. What first came to his aid was a small cheetah-like cat who charged fearlessly towards the largest serpent she had ever seen.

Ahmes sailed between Ramesses and the snake, clawing violently at the serpent as if her own life had no value. It coiled and struck at her. She quickly leapt away, and as the serpent's head hit the ground, she brought her claws down upon its eyes. Raising its tall, hooded neck high off the floor, it stared down Ramesses with pure hatred, as if it were looking through him at Ra himself. In one swift strike it attacked anew. Ramesses deftly leapt aside. Ahmes carefully balanced her offensive attacks with defensive manoeuvres to save the life of the pharaoh.

Between flashes of green scales and strikes of fangs, Ahmes saw two guards storm into the antechamber and rush to the pharaoh's side. Shaking, they planted themselves into a defensive posture. The serpent caught sight of them and rapidly slithered forward. It reared and struck down one of the guards. He withered on the floor, twisting and contorting as he burned from a fire within. In horror the other guard froze, guaranteeing his own death. Ramesses drew the dagger from the guard's scabbard. He spun and back-slashed at the serpent, grazing it across its stomach, then retreated towards the nearest door.

Apep's assailant continued to rush at the pharaoh, hindered little by the open wound. Ahmes pounced and tore her claws into its poisonous flesh, ripping through its plated armour. She retracted her claws, but one was caught on the edge of a scale. Fear slithered through her body as she pulled her paw towards her, hoping to force herself free.

The serpent turned and looked toward Ahmes. A cold, dark stare froze her to the spot. In a blur it reared back and struck down with all its power and fury, rushing at her neck.

***

Her eyes grew wide, and her soul sank with dread. Neferure did not want to complete this challenge, to fight a war between deities. An arrow of fear pierced through her courage.

In her heart she knew Apep's words were lies, though her mind could not shut out his speech. Terrified, yet captivated, she stood below the stone cold altar, grasping Akhotep's ankh in her mouth. Neferure traced the edges of the ankh with her whiskers. Her body quaked. Tremors ground her bones together. Pain gushed through her muscles, and her bite wound erupted in flame.

Through the corners of her blurry eyes, Neferure saw Sahu leading a deadly dance with the assailants of evil. He was keeping the venomous snakes from reaching her side. In her heart she knew he was giving his life to protect hers, yet her mind couldn't break free from the constricting lies Apep had coiled through her thoughts.

The monstrous serpents were pushing Sahu backwards. He was tiring, and his defences were becoming haphazard. Neferure's soul screamed for the freedom to complete her mission. Her muscles answered only to her mind, and that had become disconnected from her heart. From a remote part of her being, Neferure cried for Bast's protection, though she knew the sight of the gods was veiled.

As if in answer, the semitransparent figure of a cat appeared. With fluid grace, the cat leapt onto the broken stone, making a precise landing upon the uneven surface. It was Khu, appearing as he must have in his prime—a cat of regal dignity. His fur was again sleek, his muscles well defined, and his amulet glimmering upon his neck.

Khu glared at Apep, looking out through eyes burning with intense wisdom and resolve. Without averting his gaze he recited a spell, filling each word with power Maahes himself would have wielded. He uttered each new line with more fury than the last:

The Eye of Horus shall prevail against thee.
Death descends, O Apep,
Flee, retreat, O hated enemy of Ra,
Horus's flame drives thee from Egypt—retreat!

As Khu spoke on, Neferure could feel Apep's coils around her mind loosen. His will retreated, his grasp over her reluctantly weakening.

Several of the living stone serpents withdrew from their

fight with Sahu and redirected themselves towards Khu. They slithered around the stone wall and coiled, preparing to strike. Undaunted, Khu flawlessly finished reciting the words that the god of chaos found equal to poison:

You are slain, you are slain!
Death descends! You are slain,
Never again shall you rise!

Apep's chaotic bellow marked Khu's temporary success. Triumphant, he turned to face the serpent assailants as they struck, taunting them with his nimble maneuvers. All but one missed their mark. Khu's ghostly eyes widened in surprise as a pair of fangs sailed through his chest, hitting nothing but solid stone.

With Apep's iron chains of chaos and evil loosened, Neferure felt some control of her body. She feebly leapt towards the altar top, awkwardly landing halfway, forearms bracing her from falling and back paws scrambling wildly for a foothold. Her short reserve of strength gave out, and she fell, abandoning the ankh upon the unattainable height. Apep inched towards Akhotep's ankh. Neferure drew a deep, rattling breath and threw herself at the golden-green living metal. She centred her unsteady body upon his moving scales before clambering onto the polished hematite surface.

Neferure's tired and stinging eyes glanced to the side. The spirit of Khu had become nothing but gloomy sky. In a fury, Khesef-hra leapt over the broken wall, Tyet amulet in hand. His white linen robe was bloodied and more tattered than that of a beggar.

One of Apep's serpent guardians steadily advanced, moving into Neferure's line of sight. With a moment of renewed strength, she raised a paw and raked her claws across its crimson-black eyes, gouging through the malleable living metal.

Neferure poised herself like a sphinx, holding Akhotep's heavy ankh between her trembling paws. Frantically, she searched the skies for the exact location where Sopdet would rise. The star's appearance was soon, yet so was the revelation of The Word. Khesef-hra was mere paces from the altar, and Isis and Ra were seemingly nearing the end of their fiery argument.

Khesef-hra reached the altar and released Isis's amulet into Apep's coils. At that moment Sopdet appeared on the horizon, breaking through the storm clouds as it had in Neferure's nightmare.

A great river filled Neferure's vision as it swept through and around her, washing away the stone of Apep's temple with a blue light seemingly made of water, air, and fire. Akhotep's ankh lit up brilliantly, as if it had fallen from the moon, greatly enhancing the power that streamed past. The river of light flowed as powerfully as the Nile, yet brushed against Neferure's fur as gently as a feathered wing. Neferure looked at those around her. She could tell by their expressions that the river of light was invisible to their eyes. The others saw only decay. Through a force unseen to him, Khesef-hra was cast violently to the ground. In Neferure's ears, the voices of Isis and Ra echoed clearer than the chiming of a sistrum in the halls of Karnak.

Tiye hid behind a wall of the fading temple and pounded her fist against the disintegrating stone. Long braided hair flew into her face, and she cradled her hand. Around her lay the bodies of many stray cats. Her bodyguards were still standing, but they had scratches and bites, and one had lost an eye.

The queen of Egypt watched as Qetu, Khesef-hra, and Kesi all fled into the desert. 'Fools,' she muttered. 'They cower when there's still hope.'

The serpents Sahu had been fighting solidified into stone, then crumbled into sand. He glanced at Neferure, pride beaming in his emerald green eyes.

The unsightly stone columns of Apep's temple burned to dust and were swept away into the desert. The grotesque roof they supported crashed to the ground, vaporizing before impact. Everything of evil, of Apep, was being wiped from the earth. Overhead, the storm clouds were swept swiftly into the west. Even Neferure's illness washed away from her body, and her bite wound healed before her eyes.

Within minutes, all but Apep's altar was destroyed. It alone withstood the torrent raging around it. Neferure concentrated on directing the river of light, focusing it towards only the hematite altar. Nothing. Apep continued to resist defeat. Ra's speech paused, and Thoth's voice took its place, welling up from Neferure's unconscious mind. *'Think of yourself as a star upon the earth and the light will be drawn to you.'*

As Ra prepared to reveal The Word, Neferure concentrated on seeing herself lighting the earth with her essence. Her will was answered, and Isis's light focused towards her and the altar, shining through the centre of Akhotep's ankh. The black stone with its twisted serpent began tearing apart piece by piece. Neferure heard a hollow voice in her head.

'I am the greatest of all gods,' Apep said. 'When I have dominion over Egypt, every soul will know this.'

'So long as they define greatness as dominion,' Neferure replied.

Fear was now carved into the decaying face of the stone serpent.

'Time does not wear me down,' Apep bellowed, 'nor can any god destroy me. I will rise again and find The Word, whether during your life or when the greatness of Egypt has crumbled to myth and shattered stone. I will rise—'

The remains of the altar crashed to the ground, and the voice of Apep was silenced. Neferure fell upon the sands and dropped the ankh from her paws.

Seeing all her hopes destroyed, Tiye fled, scrambling up the Theban slope, her guards in tow. She headed back towards the city, likely weaving a tale of her innocence.

The light of the sun outshone the light of Sopdet, and Neferure's connection to the star was broken. Exhausted, she slipped out of consciousness.

The Word was heard by no one.

CHAPTER 22

The Opening of the Year

A NEW DAWN rose, casting red, purple, and orange clouds of light across the sky. The solar barque of Amun-Ra appeared again on the horizon, as it always had. Across the country, lotuses unfolded their petals, basking in the first golden rays of the new year. Shimmering metallic light cascaded through the sky, burning all shadows to dust and morning mist.

Neferure lay in the warming sands, paw-steps away from Isis's blood-red amulet. She took in slow deep breaths, filling her body with renewed life. The effects of the plague had been vanquished. Heat rushed through her muscles, and she stretched to assess her newfound strength. Clarity had returned to her mind.

Two pointy ears and a silver-furred face appeared before her line of sight. Sahu narrowed his eyes and gently batted Neferure with his paw.

Neferure gradually unearthed a well of speech from within. 'Please don't do that again.' She looked Sahu in the eye.

'Do what?' Sahu asked, tilting his face to the side and drawing back his ears.

221

'Die.'

'Oh, that.' A hint of amusement was in Sahu's voice. 'No need to worry. I've still got some lives left.'

Neferure raised her eyes. '*Some* lives?' Sahu nudged her to her feet. He retold his encounter with Meretseger and the journey given to him by a single drop of her venom.

'You met Anubis?' Neferure struggled to believe what she was hearing.

'Upuaut as well,' Sahu said. 'Ammit is certainly real. She was eyeing my heart every minute it was on the scales.'

A gust of cool wind blew from the east, swirling the fine sands. Sahu turned his head and set his gaze upon the western hills. 'I fear I shall no longer look at life through the same eyes as before I glimpsed past the veil of death.'

Neferure moved a few paw-steps closer to Sahu and brushed her head against his shoulder. 'I'm sorry for what happened, for the things I said and for allowing myself to be entranced by Apep's power.'

'You need not feel sorry.' Sahu looked back at her with kindness in his eyes. 'Few of the gods can break free from Apep's gaze. The fact that you were still able to fend off his spell as you did warrants honour. A lesser cat would have done his bidding.'

'One cat was honouring Apep's wishes,' Neferure recalled, 'and the only cat bearing an amulet who was not here was Ahmes.'

In silence Neferure and Sahu walked to rejoin the strays. Neither of them felt any immediate desire to bring Ahmes to account.

The strays were all huddled in a close group, solemnly

casting their gaze at a single focal point in the centre of their circle. Neferure sneaked around and peeked over the shoulder blades of the two shortest strays. On the ground rested the limp form of an adolescent cat. His muscles were solidly built, and even in death his face bore undaunted pride.

A ray of golden sunlight shone through Khakhati's carnelian amulet. Mehen sat before his body and gave it a single firm tap with his paw. Khakhati did not wake.

Mehen trained his eyes upon the desert ground. 'Let the gods bury him.' A soft wind caressed their fur and drew a veil of sand across Khakhati's lifeless body.

'He was skilled,' Mehen added, watching the garnet eye of Horus disappear beneath the sands. 'Arrogant and inexperienced, but honourable nonetheless.'

The strays observed a moment of silence to mourn the death of their once-foe. Khakhati's bravery and sacrifice had brought an ageless feud closer to an end.

'How will Neferure and I return to the inner city?' Sahu asked, concerning himself immediately with their remaining troubles. 'I will still be attacked by the housecats, and likely she will be as well.'

'Leave that to me.' Mehen lifted his heavy eyes to meet with Sahu's. 'I have experience sneaking into Thebes. I will take you to Karnak Temple. No cat should harm you in such a sacred place. You will have time to voice your story.'

A shrill cry pierced through the heavens, silencing Mehen's strong voice.

Out of the sky flew a falcon. He was gliding upon a golden ray of the sun, as if descending an anchor of light from Amun-Ra's solar barque. The falcon radiated majesty, larger than most of his kind and with feathers as brilliantly coloured as the painted images of Horus. He came low to the ground, levelling out and skimming the sands with the speed of an arrow. Without slowing, he clutched Isis' amulet in his sharp talons and flew off, bearing it back towards the sun.

CHAPTER 23

Per Bast

THE MANY STRONG walls of Karnak Temple protected Amun's earthly mansion: a small, secluded city in the heart of Egypt's capital. Long flags billowed freely above the stone in the clear open air, sharing the sky with a flock of ibises taking flight.

In the crowded and bustling streets below, people leapt and twirled, celebrating the new year. The resonating wail of the reed pipe, the many crystal chimes of the sistrum, the spontaneous rhythm of the lute, the divine music of harps, and rich deep drumbeats serenaded the ears of all Egyptians from dawn until dusk.

A floating jewel on the Nile, the pharaoh's ship reflected glittering light of all colours as it sailed towards Karnak. The ship spanned more than sixty feet long and was built from imported Lebanese cedar. As with all things associated with royalty, gold and precious stones were inlaid into every facet of its design. The pharaoh himself was seated on board, the crook and flail—symbols of his kingship—held tightly in hands that were crossed upon his chest. On his head rested the double crown, the white one of Upper Egypt seated within the red one of Lower Egypt. A golden cobra reared upon his brow.

In the sky above appeared an ethereal golden falcon, gliding in the morning breeze upon feathers woven of Ra's light and trailing notes of divine music as if he were a living song. The spirit-bird hovered behind the pharaoh's head, with each wing-beat wrapping his feathers around Ramesses' crown. The pharaoh listened intently to words only he seemed to hear: the voice of Horus himself. Moments later the falcon took flight again and was lost in a blur. Many cats had seen the ethereal bird, although his visitation escaped the notice of most humans. Ramesses stood up and voiced instructions to his oarsmen. Then, with deflated shoulders and eyes downcast, he gave orders to his guards. Shocked at his words, they moved to summon other nearby boats. *The Followers*, Neferure thought. *The guards had been asked to arrest the high priest, the vizier of Lower Egypt, and Queen Tiye.*

The strays met with no opposition in escorting Neferure and Sahu back to the temple, where the two would share their full story well-guarded. All trouble lay in avoiding the countless pairs of careless and exuberant human feet trampling anything beneath them. With themselves to watch out for, few cats noticed the entourage of invading strays; those who did lost sight of them quickly.

When the curtain of feet, jewels, and swirling white linen robes parted, Neferure and Sahu were free to pass unhindered down the avenue of ram-headed sphinxes. Ramesses's majestic boat was close behind. The sails were dropped, and oarsmen were navigating the vessel towards Karnak's docking quay.

Some of the temple cats caught sight of Sahu and flattened their ears, but upon sight of the strays, they did not attack. Much of the jubilant music faded once Neferure, Sahu, and their retinue passed beyond the first pylon. The notes were muted by the thick stone walls.

The familiar sight of the open-air courtyard brought Neferure a feeling of completion. Calm air and bright sunlight carried her back to a place of inner peace she had only known before Akhotep's death. Her muscles relaxed, and she exhaled tension she did not know was stored.

Two small lime-green eyes materialized from within the darkness leading into the hypostyle hall. They intently watched the newcomers, widening at the sight of Neferure. Ahmes bolted out from the gateway of the second pylon.

One stray moved forward. 'Traitor!' He hissed, fur standing on end. 'You never brought reinforcements.'

Ahmes stopped and shrunk back onto her hind paws, wide eyed. 'I don't understand. I never got any message.'

Thrashing their tails, spines arched, the strays moved to attack Ahmes, despite standing on sacred ground.

'Wait.' Neferure blocked their path. 'Evidence is against her. Still, we must let her speak.'

Tail drawn between her legs, Ahmes looked away. 'Neferure, I know you do not trust me now, but there's something I have to tell you.'

The congregation of cats listened to Ahmes recount her tale of the ankh, Takhaet's plot, the snake, and the spell she gave Khu.

'...the snake then roared—yes, *roared*—and died. To clear my head and all my senses I ran back to check on Heqaib, and then I came here to see what happened with Khu ... and the rest you know.'

Neferure waited soundlessly for the story to end. She was proud of her friend, yet the hurt of Takhaet's betrayal weighed her head to the ground.

Ahmes brushed against Neferure and purred loudly. She purred back, glad that their friendship had been restored.

'We had a similar experience,' said Neferure. 'There were snakes, a temple devoted to Apep, some kind of ghost cat who looked like a younger Khu ... and Sahu gained nine lives!'

Ahmes gaped in amazement. 'That ghost cat *was* Khu. The spell I gave him ...'

Sahu's eyes widened, and his whiskers pressed against his face. 'You mean Khu is dead?'

'No.' Ahmes pranced exuberantly upon the tips of her paws. 'He's actually awake.'

Mehen's ears perked up. 'Khu is in the temple? I had heard rumours and sought him out. I could scarcely believe, after all these years he truly is alive?'

'Yes.' Hesitating, Ahmes narrowed her eyes at Mehen. She looked to Neferure and received a nod of approval. 'If you turn to your right, he's at the end of the hypostyle hall.' She then looked to Neferure. 'Why are there strays in the city? It's a good thing Khakhati isn't here.'

Neferure closed her eyes a moment. 'Khakhati lost his life in the battle, but I'm certain he made Maahes proud.'

Sadness welled up in Ahmes' eyes.

Neferure watched Mehen wander into the depths of the hypostyle hall, bearing on his face the look of one returning home after a long journey. With unhurried steps, Neferure followed, plodding past the second pylon and into the depths of the great stone-columned hall. Sahu was stuck behind in the courtyard recounting the details of their quest, speaking of divine battles, and answering many questions.

Both father and son could be seen in the distance as dark silhouettes: one a frail heap of tangled fur and the other a powerfully built cat assuming a noticeably subservient posture. Mehen said nothing; his right ear swivelled in Neferure's direction.

As she grew closer, Neferure noticed that Khu had obtained a fresh scar exactly where the snake fangs had pierced his ethereal form.

Khu raised his vibrant green eyes to look at Neferure. 'I believe that the spell worked.'

Neferure looked briefly at Mehen, who did not return the glance. 'Back in the desert,' she began, looking again at Khu, 'how did you do all of that?'

Khu's bright eyes twinkled. 'Thoth gave me the wisdom to learn to travel in spirit. You can't expect my ageing form to keep me from battling the evils that threaten Egypt, now can you?'

'Truly of the lines of Maahes,' echoed Sahu's voice as he entered the hall. He trotted past the many columns until he reached the wall, and there he settled beside Neferure.

Khu looked directly at his son. 'Maahes has decided that due to your recent acts of selfless devotion to this land and to its inhabitants, you shall be made an honorary member of my lineage. I now see clearer into the minds of the gods. Had I gone against Maahes's wisdom and initiated you during your youth, you would never have rebelled and risen to the position only you could command. Truly, there are many mysteries that we fail to see until the end.'

Khu drew a slow, deep, rattling breath. 'Neferure, now that you are here, there is something I must ask. I have completed what I was born to do. My time in Egypt will not be long, and I will soon journey towards Amenti. I ask that you continue along the path of wisdom on which Thoth started me. The knowledge will seem complex at first, but the god of science and mysteries surely has more to teach you so that your full strengths can be realized.'

Neferure and Sahu exchanged glances; becoming a pupil of a great god was usually a path reserved for cats of lineage and was often filled with much difficulty. Neferure was not sure she was ready or able to walk down such a path. 'I will do my best, but you must tell me how.'

Khu sat up onto his hind paws. He moved slowly and with immense struggle, as if gravity itself was the greatest enemy he'd ever faced. Wholly withdrawn into his own mind, he seemed not to have heard Neferure's question.

'For twenty-one years,' Khu said, 'I've cheated death and always won. Now the game turns against me, as it must and always will.' He paused to take another deep rattling breath. Mehen settled into a regal pose, though his gaze remained fixed upon the ground. The storm in his eyes had settled into a long-hidden grief. 'Remember this: we are as shooting stars drawn to the earth, veering for a moment, spending a lifetime, and then passing from earthly view to a new and distant fate.'

Neferure again exchanged glances with Sahu. That had hardly been the answer she'd expected.

'Despite what you may believe,' Mehen said, looking up, 'my father *has* been this rhetorical his whole life.'

A soft meow echoed through the hypostyle hall. Neferure turned around and saw Ramesses standing in full regalia along the walkway near the second pylon, where the sun filtered in before being lost to the forest of columns. In the shadows behind him stood two priests wearing plain white robes. They were each holding a small, heavily adorned chest. Neferure found the sight unusual, yet it still did not account for the meow. Ahmes emerged from behind a column and wrapped herself around Ramesses's feet, purring and entangling herself in his long linen robes.

Ramesses motioned for Neferure and Sahu to move forward. 'Come, children of Bast.' His voice resonated through the temple.

Neferure and Sahu, in a way quite uncustomary for cats, listened. Mehen followed them through the columns and onto the walkway. Khu remained behind, yet watched the proceedings intently.

Neferure and Sahu sat in front of him. 'Let it be known that from this point forward, you and your chosen descendants shall bear the title of Per-Bast, for of all cats who ever walked in Egypt, her essence beats strongest in your hearts.'

The two priests emerged from the background and flanked the pharaoh on each side. They opened the adorned chests and presented them. From the chest to his right,

Ramesses removed a meticulously crafted usekh collar, strung with a row of garnet beads atop a row of turquoise stones. Separating those rows of long oval beads were rows of small round, highly polished golden balls. In the centre of the collar rested an exquisite scarab of lapis lazuli and gold, holding up a garnet solar disc. Two resplendent wings, feathered in all three stones, arched upwards to carry the garnet sun. Gold outlined every detail of the amulet.

Ramesses affixed the usekh collar around Neferure's neck. 'You, and all those of Per-Bast to follow, shall bear the amulet of the scarab, an emblem of the rising sun, for it is by your doing that it continues to rise.' He then removed an identical usekh collar from the opposite chest and placed it upon Sahu. 'The duty of your lineage is to protect your kindred and guard Egypt as Bast would her own children.'

Neferure's heart swelled with joy. She and Sahu had been awarded the greatest honour possible among cats, yet she could already feel the heavy weight of the polished stones and golden beads bearing down upon her shoulder blades.

Sahu shifted his muscles beneath his usekh collar, adapting himself as best he could to his new adornment.

The pharaoh gave a slight smile and departed towards his boat. 'Come' He spoke lightly, and without looking back. 'They will be waiting.'

With the bright sun on their backs, Neferure and Sahu passed through the towering obelisks and pylons, following Ramesses as he met with his retinue and exited Karnak. The pharaoh and his guard passed down the avenue of Amun's majestic ram-headed sphinxes toward the jewelled boat awaiting them.

Neferure looked over at Sahu. He nuzzled her and then stood, beckoning her to follow. Together they headed towards the growing congregation of cats who were meowing loudly outside the temple, waiting to hear their tale. One kitten leapt onto a stone sphinx to gain a greater view, fascination beaming in his young eyes.

Glossary

Aaru—The reed fields, the paradise of the afterlife. Aaru was considered to be an idyllic version of life as it had been in Egypt.

Amenti—The realm of the dead. Inhabited by gods such as Osiris, Thoth, and Anubis, as well as many supernatural beings and demon-like creatures. The dead had to pass the many gates and trials before having their hearts weighed against a feather. Those who passed were granted eternal life in Aaru.

Ammit—A demon with the head of a lioness, the body of a crocodile and the hind of a hippopotamus. She devoured the hearts of those who did not have the purity to enter into Amenti.

Amun-Ra—The sun god. Every day he sailed over Egypt in his solar barque. At night he sailed through the underworld and fought his enemy, the serpent Apep.

Anubis—A jackal god who assisted in the 'weighing of the heart' ceremony. He also watched over embalming rituals and guarded the tombs from thieves.

Apep—A large serpentine demon. He was the bringer of primeval chaos and evil. Every day he sought to devour Amun-Ra's solar barque as the sun god sailed past the twelve gates of the underworld.

Bast—A feline deity appearing as a housecat. She was seen as a great mother who guarded Egypt, cats, and women just as a mother cat guarded her kittens. Bast was said to be the daughter of Ra. She embodied the life-giving qualities of the sun. In later times a grand temple, with a sacred grove, was built in her honour and was host to ritualistic parties.

Hall of Two-Truths—The hall containing the great scale with which Anubis weighed the hearts of those seeking eternal life.

Horus—The falcon god who was the son of Isis and Osiris. In myth he ruled over Egypt after his father had died. The pharaoh was viewed as a living embodiment of Horus.

Isis—The wife of Osiris and the mother of Horus, said to be the wisest of the gods. She was powerful at magic and her breath was life-giving. Frequently she was portrayed protecting royalty with her outstretched wings.

Karnak—A grand temple complex built primarily for the honour of Amun-Ra. Always growing, construction spanned from the Middle Kingdom through to the Ptolemaic period.

Khepri—Scarab god of the rising sun. He symbolized renewal and resurrection. He was seen pushing the sun across the sky just as a scarab would roll a pile of dung containing its eggs.

Khonsu—Worshipped in Thebes as a lunar deity. Son of Amun and Mut.

Luxor—A smaller temple complex to the south of Karnak.

Maahes—The lion god of war who protected the pharaoh in battle. He also defended Amun-Ra's solar barque against the serpent Apep and protected those who were innocent while he punished the betrayers of Ma'at.

Ma'at—Winged goddess who represented order, truth and justice—the very things that kept chaos and disorder from overtaking the land. The heart of the deceased was weighed against a single feather of hers before passing into Amenti.

Mafdet—A cat goddess who offered protection against scorpions, snakes and other threatening creatures. Those who were bitten or stung often invoked Mafdet's healing powers through rituals.

Meretseger—Known as 'She Who Loves Silence.' A cobra goddess who guarded the tombs on the Western Bank of Thebes.

Mut—A mother goddess and the wife of Amun-Ra.

Osiris—Ruler of Amenti, husband to Isis, and father to Horus. He judged the dead before they were deemed worthy to live eternally. He ruled for a time in Egypt before being killed by his brother. The magic and devotion of Isis brought him back to life in the afterlife.

Sekhmet—A lioness goddess responsible for nearly destroying the human race. Plagues and diseases were often blamed on her wrath, and her healing powers were invoked to dispel them. She destroyed the pharaoh's enemies and embodied the destructive aspect of the sun.

Sistrum—A metal instrument consisting of a frame and longitudinal metal rods. When shook it produced a clear chiming noise.

Sopdet—Isis's star, known nowadays as Sirius. Sopdet travelled through the sky following the constellation of Osiris (Orion's belt). Sopdet was hidden for seventy days of the year. The day the star appeared again on the horizon marked the new year and the beginning of the Nile's flood season.

Tyet Amulet—A symbol of the goddess Isis. The amulet was shaped like an ankh, but with downward arms, and also known as the 'Knot of Isis'. Was seen to represent resurrection and eternal life.

Thoth—The god of wisdom, writing, architecture, and science. He frequently appeared as an ibis or a man with the head of an ibis.

Udjat—The right eye of Horus. An udjat amulet was seen to have protective and healing powers.

Upuaut—The 'Opener of the Way.' A jackal god who led the deceased through the underworld and protected them while on their journey.

Uraeus—An amulet of a rearing serpent. The uraeus was worn on the pharaoh's crown and was seen as an emblem of kingship.

Usekh Collar—A necklace consisting of multiple rows of stone, glass, or gold beads. Amulets were often strung onto such collars.

Author Bio

LARA-DAWN STIEGLER is a Canadian author who was born and raised in Vancouver, Canada. She has had an enduring interest in the connection between humanity and nature, and the cultures that exonerated that bond. Inspiration for her writing comes from research into the past and from her affinity for animals. *Per-Bast: A Tale of Cats in Ancient Egypt* is her debut novel.

www.laradawn.com